Basements
and
Other Museums

Basements
and
Other Museums

Vedran Husić

Black
Lawrence
Press

Black
Lawrence
Press

www.blacklawrence.com

Executive Editor: Diane Goettel
Cover Design: Heather McGuire
Cover Art: "East Facing" by Heather McGuire
Book Design: Amy Freels

Published 2018 by Black Lawrence Press.
Printed in the United States.

To Naira

Contents

A Brief History of the Southern Slavs

They knelt upon the land, unable to walk any longer, blessed the ground, named the river, flourished and multiplied, had a God for each season, then had only one God, the winter God, broke their faith upon a stone, divided the tribe, died standing up, hid in the hills from tax collectors, slept fitfully through dreamless nights, grew cunning, reaped the harvest, raised pigs, turned landlords when there wasn't war, passed down in song how they lived, how they suffered, how they were trodden upon but overcame, rebelled against kings, rebelled against the weather, against the heights of mountains, and what stood beyond, their divided blood, formed a state, fought a war, fought another, fought one more, were invaded, were enlightened, were betrayed, wore progressive shoes, put on reactionary hats, whispered in the presence of books, became prisoners of ideas, then arrogant like all nonbelievers, then violent like all who regain their faith.

I hear, the axe has bloomed,
I hear, the place is not nameable,
I hear, they call life
our only refuge.
—*Paul Celan, "I Hear, the axe has bloomed"*

Deathwinked

We called sniper alley the alley of wolves. We were young and boys and had nicknames for everything, first of all the girls. There was the Nanny, the Epilogue, and the Soulcrusher. We thought these nicknames very clever, breathless with truth. We were thirteen and easily excited. To be killed by a sniper meant to be deathwinked, a verb. I came up with that. I had a minimum understanding of poetry, a maximum amount of fear.

We ran across the alley of wolves to test our recent manhood, among other things. We ran because there was nothing better to do. We ran because it was more bearable than standing still. We were young and anxious to be brave. We were practicing martyrs. Our fathers were gone; mine gone forever, heaven-swallowed one winter night at the front. Miralem's father was still at the front, firing his gun at the threatening distance. All three of us dreamed of soldierhood and feared that the war would soon run out. Edin's father had come back from the front and was gone in yet another way, halfway between the gone of Miralem's father and the never coming back of my father. He was crazy, according to the completely not insane. He spoke the names of the dead, but not in his sleep, like normal people. He confused the living for the dead, which worried the living. We all smiled at him and pitied him the best we could. We smiled at him and measured our sanity against his truth. Edin took it all in stride, in run, explaining it away through philosophy, intellectualizing the problem until the problem grew wings. His father's rants did not bother him, but it bothered his family, who wanted to institutionalize the father. But there were no institutions left. Edin argued that to call somebody insane was ridiculous in time of war. Nobody in his family listened to him; he was thirteen, which is its own form of insanity.

Our fathers were gone, and our mothers had no authority over us. We loved them, our unreluctant Slavic mothers, but we loved our courage more. "War is our true mother," Edin once said, inspired and dumbfounded. "Unable to give birth, men make war," he said another time. Edin was the oldest by a month, a small lifetime, had slow blue eyes, and spoke deliberately, like a drunk wanting to be understood. He liked Kierkegaard; he liked the idea of Kierkegaard. He argued about religion, for and against it. His father had taught philosophy and was now insane, or within untiring reach of insanity. His family had been wealthy, but now money did not matter, had lost meaning. It was wartime and everything was free, and everybody on the eastern side of Mostar was equal as the dead are equal. The dream of communism bloomed among casual shell bursts and articulate sniper fire, on the eastern side of a town without bridges.

Eastsiders have nothing to lose but their lives, and an afterworld to gain. Alley-runners of all countries unite!

The family library lay in rubble, but some of the books had been saved, and being the only books left, they were many times read and meticulously understood by Edin. Edin came up with the name "alley of wolves" and it had been his idea to run across it. To impress the Epilogue more than anything else. Larger reasons became apparent only later, and by virtue of their late arrival sounded like excuses. Ideas were Edin's guardian angels; he had a whole tear-bright choir of them. Beyond the grave there will be singing. He had bulletproof testosterone. A missionary's courage. There were doubters to convert to something less than doubt. There were detractors to prove wrong. And death proved everybody wrong, eventually, always. We congregated near a spilling set of trashcans, behind buildings bruised by mortar fire. Houses in every state of uninhabitable lined the alley on one side, walls left to stand as monuments to futility, while on the other side stood nothing, open space and a gravel path sloping toward the river. And up ahead, the nothing-goal, more desolated houses and the mute storefronts of empty shops, and the stone remains of a mosque, with its third of a minaret, and the promise of intermission and the burden, almost motherly, of the run back. A small and narrow street, strewn with garbage and garbage-scented, our ground of play. These adjectives come easy, self-compounded at birth.

Mostar, my city, you are far from me now, but I peek through the spyglass and you appear so near. In my third-floor apartment, in the neverdesperate America of my childhood dreams, at my desk, armed with pencil and paper, sensitive as a landmine, fumbling similes like live grenades, I, the young, triple-tongued poet, write down the name of my birthcity like the name of a former lover. Mostar. Mostar, my city, stunned quiet. They took the Most, threw it into the river and made you unnamable. My city, one night you went dark all around me. You trembled and could not be embraced. The bombs fell on you, near constant and heartbeatloud. I recommend war-tourism to any artist, poet especially, a month or so of up-close death, a month, or twenty-three, of dark-houred explosions in a world maddened by sirens. You'll never lack material, or have to account for sudden mood swings, and you'll never lose at those drunken games between friends, intimate games, those poetic games of whosufferedmost.

Three floors are enough to kill a man. The truthhearing poet gives the truthsharpened tip of his pencil a lick, he writes: Three floors are enough to kill a man/There can be no hate without memory/To love is to imagine/In the white noise of other feelings. That with his pencil the poet writes the truth is implied, was implied, is implied no longer. He gives the pencil another swift lick, he writes: All children pretend/Their games are serious/All games have rules/Even the games of animals/ Have rules. Our game had but a few rules. If you ran last yesterday, you must run first today. That was one rule. If you ran across the alley to the other side, you must run back. That was rule number two, for there was another way back, sniper-less but long. And there were rules of which we were ignorant, the secret rules of the sniper. But whether the sniper followed any rules was left to debate. Sundays we did not run. Yesterday, Miralem had run last; he would run first today. Who would run second was decided by a coin toss. Edin would run second. I, last. Tomorrow I would run first. Tomorrow I would not run.

The time leading up to the first run was the happiest time of the day, our concentration lax, our muscles fearful and limber, the words between us intimate, unexpected, binding. Sometimes we sang. It was morning, during the week of lentil soup. Miralem stretched his arms and legs, while Edin and I sat on opposing stubs of stone arguing in war-hushed tones. The blue sky promised no rain, and the sun looked a blotchy and vague yellow. Miralem threw one arm behind his back and pressed the bent elbow with his other hand, his legs wide apart, his torso stout and armless. The amber sheen of autumn leaves, the gazelle-like wind, the abashed leaf-rustle, they all spoke in different languages about the same things. Beauty. Nature. Truth. Poetry. We spoke of philosophy, Edin and I, while Miralem quietly and thoughtfully stretched, and in the new dawn's unraveling silence, under a sky morningpureblue, the sniper fired the first shot of a long day. Bullet, trashcan, a metal *ping* almost adorable, almost loud. We turned our heads toward the sound, then toward each other, then back. We resumed our conversation and Miralem joined us. He was arguably pretty, one of those who narrowed their eyes when they grinned, one of those who gestured with their fists. His eyes were green, a little blue, and he had a full Slavic forehead, broad and thought-pale. He was short but athletic; he was short and had a temper. He did not like tall girls. He did not like the Soulcrusher, with whom I played games in death-proof basements. There we spoiled each other for our future selves. He brought daily lilies for the Nanny and kissed her deeply, with a more meaningful tongue, with more daring and saliva than I ever did Selma. I write her name like the name of something lost. She knew how to swing the hips she did not have. She knew how to haggle good enough and long enough to make you give up everything. With her smile she fooled you into laughing at yourself. With her laughing eyes she crushed your soul. She dreamed of a husband with money. She dreamed of big hips. A skirtful of memories, everything I have, for a handful of her skirt.

Miralem had played soccer before the war, before the cemetery turn of every idle field, before the dead packed stadiums; he was fast, his run was urgent and blind, it was a sprint, and he ran with his head down. And yesterday he'd tripped and fallen a yard or so from safety. The sniper had fired and missed. He did not fire again. A little dust rose, it settled. Miralem was on the other side by then, bent over, with his hands on his knees, breathing greedily. He did not fire again as if to let us take in the full magnitude of his miss, or to impress us with his patience. The confidence of those with death on their side, how could we ever understand it? Miralem said nothing when we got to him, his tender calm edging on some kind of bewilderment, and after the run back, we walked home in silence, and parted from each other in silence, the silence of raised stakes. Now Miralem ridiculed the sniper, saying that he missed because he was a bad shot, and not on purpose, saying he was some fat, pimply boy playing at war, and not a man of many battles, not a man at all, just a novice at death and not worth the fantasy of our revenge. But Edin wouldn't have it. No, to him he was a man and a master, a Machiavellian sniper prince, with a nihilist's love of beauty; his aim is steady and true, he shoots you with a shot made of lead, his slit eye is Catholic blue. Edin had read his Celan, saved from the rubble. Death is a master from the Balkans. But it is more intimate than that. He is a close relation, the mysterious uncle bearing strange gifts at each prophetic visit, the one who winks at you behind your parent's back. We were brought up on his knee, on the black milk of his wisdom. Our blood is his blood. The one who waltzes you across the alley of wolves, the one who lets you stand on his feet as you move against each other in this gently wicked dance. Our songs are his songs. He sings into your hair as you dance. He whispers in your ear, forbids you to stop.

Miralem ran across the alley, with his head down, with his head only slightly lifted toward the end. Alive on the other side, he grinned at us, his eyes almost closed. Then it was gone, the grin, memory-wiped, collapsed into a thinking pout. The sniper had not fired. Sometimes he didn't. And when he didn't he blessed our run with innocence, like running before the war. Sometimes that was what we wanted. We had run for a month now, had been in this war for years, and weren't getting any wiser. So why not go back? To a time of sparrow-enswirled minarets and non-firewood lindens, to a time of packed café terraces and their murmur like rushing water, when death and its mirror image, life in war, were as distant as nightmares after waking. In front of our buildings, punched blue and black by rockets, was a large courtyard, and this courtyard had been the setting of our first game, a game of collection. Under the spell of sunlight and tall grass, we'd search for bullet shells and find also glinting syringes, uncapped bottles of pills, an occasional limb abstracted from the body. One day, we found a mortar shell the size of a baby seal, unexploded. We dared each other to touch it. Edin moved toward it, extending an unsteady finger. "BOOM," Miralem yelled at the point of contact, and Edin jumped back. Miralem laughed and Edin fumed. They fought it out, and afterwards both fumed. And as they sat on opposite sides of the projectile, not looking at each other, I got up from my seat and placed my palm against its belly. The metal was scorched by the sun and felt smooth and naked to the touch. I let my fingers linger haughtily, waiting for them to notice. I felt an upward rush of courage, like a declaration. Miralem and Edin joined me, our three hands pressed against the hot metal in a silent oath. That was when we knew we wanted to be soldiers and never die.

Beyond the broken-down stores and houses, beyond the kneeling minaret, on the side that we first ran to reach, was their headquarters, in the sandbagged gymnasium of a shell-bitten and nearly roofless elementary school. We peeked on three soldiers, all three young; we watched them gather by a corner table, watched two of them sit on upturned milk crates and the other stand; watched them eat lentil soup from a can that was warmed by old-fashioned fire; watched them listen to a portable radio as they ate with no hope of satiation; watched their hands busily scratch and their lips seldom move; watched all three turn toward the radio when the human voice got lost behind an unrelenting tearing of sandpaper. The soldiers went back to patrol the rubble and we watched them walk away, toward danger, unafraid and amused. There was something solemn about their amusement, something sensual and elusive about the way they carried themselves, in their warstained boots and burden-heavy uniforms, something eerily casual about the guns slung over their shoulders, lustful and sentimental about their lack of helmets. What bleak respect we had for them, all God-like and dusty-loined. They were not so much defenders of our city as defenders of our dream of the city. The odds were against them, but the crowd on their side, the cheer of the wind in the trees.

We wandered about for a while, wasting time before our run back. It was getting to be noon, the shadows growing long and ragged. Women appeared on the street, braving their way to market located makeshift in one of the rear classrooms, smuggled goods. Once, we had looked for ingredients to make a cake for my birthday and found nothing but a nestful of eggs. We had the party in a basement, with no cake, but with many candles, more than was my age. In another yard, a new breed of child explorers rummaged for shells in the overgrown grass, their pockets full of singing. Farther east, toward Stolac, a blue-gray tower of smoke had risen, straying from its origin, swallowing houses whole along its path. We saw the absence of the bridge and a gentle curve of river below. The Old Bridge was gone, but the Neretva River was still here, flowing bright and prewar green. The river doesn't care. The river has seen worse. The river is not concerned with what we throw in it: debris, bodies, blood, and stone, the water stitches it all to a mend, never stopping to wonder what we send downriverflowing. We climbed a garage and flopped down on our bellies. With our voices love-timid, our stares remote, we looked over our half of the city. Behind us, the boughs of a large tree whose name we had not yet learned shielded us from danger. Green mountains and hills enclosed us on all sides, separating us from our enemies but not from ourselves. The piled smoke rose still higher, spread out greater than a cathedral, more clouded than the idea of God. Sparrows chirped, crests chirped, gunfire chirped. The waxwing had flown south, summer was over. The dandelions had been beheaded; the lilies had hanged themselves. It was autumn now and nothing bloomed, except the yearlong ax.

Miralem was on the starting side again, alive and well and one day braver, while Edin stood on the edge of safety, waiting to run. He stood just behind a little shop, its interior gray and plundered. Before the war, I'd run there to get emergency Vegeta for my mother, and sometimes its owner, old and Hellenic Mr. Salemović, would call me into the back and ask me to stack some items for him, rewarding my impromptu work with free candy. I remember red jars of Ajvar, tall glass bottles of Laro Juice, and those compact silver cans of Eva Sardines, with a waving walrus dressed as a sailor on the blue cover. I remember Dorina Chocolates and Bananko Bars, Bajadera Pralines and Napolitanke Wafers, and Jaffa Cookies with their chocolate skins and orange jelly hearts. I remember a balance scale on the counter, with numerous dust-colored weights in increasing sizes of mass; I remember the slow sway of its thin shoulders, the delicate movements of its plates, their eventual, hard-earned symmetry. One surging whiff of Vegeta and I'm back in a light-filled kitchen, beside my mother who smells of red vegetables and spices, standing innocently in the way and marveling at her instinctual measurements. Just one whiff and I remember my mother, half-orphaned by one war, wholly widowed by another, tasting the sauce and smiling down at me her expert opinion. Music comes from the living room, where my father is taking his afternoon nap. This tells me that we already ate, that the food being prepared is for tomorrow, that despite the Sunday texture of this memory, this is more likely a work day, a day my mother will end at the hospital, where she will begin the new day, working at her typewriter, giving injections, changing sheets. The number of coffee cups on the table tells me there will be guests, our next-door neighbors, a Catholic man who always guessed the card in my hand and his Muslim wife who could read the future in the muddy remnants of the coffee.

Edin stood on the brink of danger, waiting to prove his bravery. But in war everybody is brave, even the coward. Even the sniper at his post, beguiling the fates. The three soldiers patrolling the rubble, they were braving another day of boredom, their courage doomed. Huddled around the radio, they waited for the news to tell them what they already knew. The war will not end today. The children in the tall grass, in the bloom of their inexperience, they were brave without knowing. The women in search of food, carrying their grief inside them like a long pregnancy, their bravery no conciliation for their loss. Everybody is brave in wartime. Everybody wise, even the fool with his warning. We were just braver, the answered prayers of our patient tormenters. Victims of our own death-mined wisdom. Strange prideful lambs, we made our courage our God. Like every rose is a flower, every Slav boy is an Icarus.

Edin was on the verge of his run, waiting for a favorable sign that only he knew how to tell. Then, suddenly, he was off, his footsteps echoing bluntly in the empty street, his thin vicious elbows stabbing the air behind him. The sniper fired and Edin crashed to the soundless asphalt.

Deathwinked.

I thought I screamed, I thought I tore my mouth with my voice, but my cry, its angular fury, was only imagined. I took a couple of steps toward Edin, to soothe the distance between us, but Miralem raised his palm and I obeyed. We looked on from the disbelief of safety, looked at his unflinching body, waiting for loyalty to move us, for fear to release us, for courage to break us free. I wiped my tears on my sleeve; I looked at Miralem and knew. He lowered his hand and we ran. A new game had begun, a game of retrieval. I grabbed Edin under his armpits and

Miralem grabbed him by his ankles. We carried Edin home, running. The sun was in my eyes; I thought I would trip. I felt the weight of his body like never before. The sniper did not fire.

And now? What now? Why stop one's war story in mid-exhalation? Why bring in the present to take revenge on the past? The past, which is our only refuge. Now my sleep is fragmented by nightmares. Now I'm ghost-weary, my tongue a cripple. Now I lean out of my window and think about ending this chance-riddled life, but can never keep my eyes closed long enough. Now I walk barefoot in my dark apartment trying to catch in a mason jar every flicker of my insanity. Now I sit at my desk and write.

The sniper did not fire.

Now that the war is over we laugh that it ever began. But even now we hunger for the right man to lead us down the wrong path again. For even now, in some small, divided village, a Milošević is waiting to be stubbornly born.

Now the exhumed graves are again silenced with our soil.

Now the past is burned like sheets of infidelity.

Now, in comfortable prisons, under supervision kind and condescending, sworn enemies bond over a game of cards.

Documentary

Haris H.

Only a delusional man will seek solace and affirmation from his memories, but I'm telling you the past is all I have, all I know, when talking about him, and there is a kind of solace, if not affirmation, in thinking back on our shared childhood in America. I came to the pool the day after we moved into our new apartment, thirteen, skinny, shy, white as bread, with very little English and speaking Bosnian with a German accent that Dario picked up on right away because he had lived there, too. He came up to me, drops of water tracing his chest, asking me to join the others at the table by the gate. By *others* he meant the other Bosnians living in our apartment complex in the suburbs of St. Louis, two other boys and three girls. We hung out together a lot. To ask me now if I knew then what that kid would be capable of as a man is ridiculous, but even then he was strange, though it's hard to explain. He was a loner in a sense, but he had a lot of friends, too. Everybody knew him, and everybody liked him. He was nice, he made sure he was nice. He was funny and handsome and he could talk to you without making you feel like you had to work for it, his interest and attention, and that was part of his charm. Introspection did not make him somber or keep him in his room like it did me when we were older. He was always out, but he was always high or drunk when he went, and eventually I thought this was the only way he could take it, going out with friends he had less and less in common with, the talking, the niceness. He showed a bitter disinterest in talking about the war, this I noticed right away. His experience of it was similar to mine, uneventful, although his father was in a concentration camp for a couple of years. But Dario was too young, I think, to really have felt the impact of that absence or remember much of anything about the war except the basements and the fireworks. Like me, he came from a mixed background; his father was a non-practicing Muslim, his mother Orthodox and religious in a minor way. Crossing herself before a plane ride, praying for a good doctor visit, that's how Dario described it. I remember her as a nervous woman, shy smiles and sudden laughter, questioning every noise in the night, jumping off her seat at thunder, unable to stand the car alarms it set off in our neighborhood. I think religion helped her cope like cleaning the house helped mine. It was only after the incident at the bar that I started to wonder what it meant for Dario having a mother who was Orthodox, a Serb in other people's words. But I don't think that had anything to do with what happened in Los Angeles, or else we'd all be murderers.

Dina K.

I took a creative writing class the second semester of my sophomore year and that's where we met. He was the TA, but

I should tell you that nothing happened between us until after
the semester ended. I remember coming into the room—he was
already there, writing his name on the board—and sitting down
between these two girls in the back who were eagerly waiting
for him to finish because they'd been guessing since he came
in what his ethnicity was. The one on my right thought he was
Mexican-American, which was plausible since he was dark-toned
and we were in Arizona, but the one on the left, thinking that
he was still too white and hearing a slight accent when he asked
how everybody was doing, thought he was Greek, born on some
forlorn island in the Aegean, a fisherman in his youth. Once the
name was on the board, I knew he was like me, from a country
neither of my flanking classmates had ever heard of. Dario loved
it when I told him this story. The three of us would talk to him
after class, asking him about character and point-of-view just
to have something to talk to him about. Eventually it was just
me who accompanied him to his office, which was in the same
building as my next class, and we would talk less and less about
writing and more about our personal lives. It may have looked
like flirting, but the way Dario talked to you, that charm of his,
you would have to be his sister for it not to look like flirting.
He even flirted with the boys if you ask me. After my story was
workshopped, I told him it would only be fair now to read a story
of his, but he said it would mess up the learning process because
after reading one of his stories I wouldn't trust anything he had
to say about writing. Self-deprecation was part of his charm. It
was only after our last class that he gave me a story of his, and all
the attraction I had for him seemed validated by his writing. As
soon as I finished reading it, I burst into tears. He would have
hated having my tears be a measure of the story's quality, but I

did cry and I did find it beautiful. I don't think I'm much of a writer, but I'm a good reader, and Dario even told me once how highly he thought of my write-ups, my instinct for recognizing authenticity in a character, which he said was what's most important in a story, having authentic characters. His characters were definitely authentic and I knew what I felt was right, that it was a wonderful story and I was in love with its writer.

Haris H.

So Bosnia played Serbia in a World Cup qualifier and Dario thought it would be fun to get the whole gang together again and go watch the game in one of those bars that line Gravois in South City. Really, it was about reuniting me with the others, because I was the one who had lost touch—such a nice, evocative phrase—with everyone after high school. My only link, however tenuous, was Dario, who visited me in my room to exchange books and talk about what we were reading. Sometimes we talked about what we were writing or wanted to write in vague, roundabout ways. Talk only, because he never let me read what he had written, because he was embarrassed by it, he said, because he did not want to show it to anybody until it was perfect, which I thought was bullshit on multiple levels. Thinking about it now, I should have pressed him more, because it could have given me some new insight. Maybe I wouldn't feel as lost as I feel now. Or is that just a fantasy, not the notion of the artist baring his soul between the lines, but the idea of a knowable soul? So he would come by from time to time, or we'd go out together on those rare occasions when I felt like going out or didn't have too much schoolwork. We were attending different colleges in the area, both of us majoring in English. On those nights out, I requested we go to an American place and that he only bring Aida along. Yet when he invited me to the game, I said yes for some reason. We were no longer inseparable; we were no longer Neal and Jack, as we used to call ourselves after we read *On the Road*, alternating the names between each other, deluding ourselves we were writers and American. We were no longer inseparable but I still needed him as a friend, because he was the only one I had who could understand the reality of my past as well as the dream of my future. That's if the past has any reality at all, especially a shared past? Maybe the smell of wet cement in the summer heat that was the smell of the pool more so than chlorine. Or the fried egg smell of faucet water we greedily drank out of our cupped grimy hands after playing outside for hours. Anyway, so I came into Bar Mostar, where I hadn't stepped foot in for years, and Franko, the owner, a friend of my father's, grabbed at his heart with a feigned grimace. More mocking gestures of surprise came from the men sitting at the bar, old friends from high school, some of them still calling me professor because I used to wear reading glasses in class. The professor has returned from a long sabbatical, they shouted, or one shouted and the rest repeated, and I smiled at them with enough pity that they'd realize I pitied them and just walked on by, leaving them sitting on their bar stools hunched over like apes. I really don't hold a grudge against any of them, but just by that small interaction with the past I knew I shouldn't have come. And Dario didn't help the situation. By his dumb smile, I could tell he was high. But even in that dumb smile there lurked something ironic and bitter that never let you know exactly where you stood with him.

Dina K.

After I read his story, we went to a café near my dorm to talk about it and later we went in his car to get a bite at a place close to where he lived, which was off campus, more rundown, and predominantly Latino. Afterwards we went to his house and had sex on the couch in his living room. That summer, after he came back from St. Louis, we started seeing each other again. Since I'm from North Phoenix, I invited him once to dinner because he was saying how much he missed Bosnian cooking. The only thing I ever made was pasta, which I would cook a big pot of that would last me for the week. It was then, as we sat around the dinner table, while my mother was toasting to our health, skinny shot glasses of šljivovica held in the air, that I realized how absurd his coming was. Dario was already dating Laura at that time, and here I was introducing him to my parents, as a friend, of course, but still. The one time we talked about her he told me how much he wanted to get out of the relationship but didn't want to antagonize her and her friends, who were his friends too, since they were all in the same program. That was the word he used, antagonize. I didn't feel particularly sorry for her—I do now, of course—and I would be lying if I said that I didn't enjoy what we did. There was always the undercurrent of danger, which made every touch more exhilarating. I was young enough and strong enough to love without being loved back, to not expect and want anything more than temporary pleasures. I couldn't do that now. We were together for about a year and I never once spent the night in his apartment. We talked, had sex, ate, talked some more, had sex again, all in an afternoon, and then I would leave before dusk thinking that we were both happy. Early on he asked me, maybe confusing my intuition for experience, how many lovers I had before him. Dario said words like lover and artist, lovemaking and affairs, without being at all self-conscious. I told him the truth, that he was only my second. Then I asked him what I promised myself never to ask, and he told me that he didn't know, that he'd never kept count, and so he went through each one of them, from the first, at thirteen, to the last, which was me. It didn't feel like bragging, because he told me about them in such a solemn tone of voice and because there was something very vulnerable about his nakedness that day, his body laid out straight on the twin bed, legs crossed at the ankle, his hands behind his head making wings of his thin, muscular arms, a band of light crossing his stomach like a magic trick. Many of them were one-night stands, some he went to high school with, some were older, some married, some had children with whom he played while their mothers were in the kitchen or the shower, some were Bosnian, some not, some black and some white, and some he never saw again in his life. About the girl he had the longest relationship with, he only said that she was Bosnian. I asked him to tell me more about her and he smiled, telling me that their lovemaking once they started dating was never as good as it was while they were sneaking around like we were doing now. I asked if he had loved her and he said he did, until the end. Then I asked him why they broke up and he said because she feared that she loved him more than he loved her, and that even though he feared he would lose her if he didn't prove her wrong, he feared proving her wrong more. He said this with such quickness and fluency it felt pre-prepared, as though he'd taken it out of one of his stories, learned it by heart like the Browning and Keats he would recite to me in bed, eyes closed, with the gravity of prayer.

Haris H.

You know, I don't think I have made myself fully understood, and I have such a desperate need to be understood. Maybe you should talk to Aida, though I don't think she will want to talk to you. Their relationship was odd. She and I actually dated for a while, almost all of sophomore year, so I know what she's like, a bit demanding, even needy. And though she was smart, she got so easily distracted by her thoughts, and it took me a while to realize it wasn't a performance, as Dario had also thought, just her natural habit, though that didn't make the theatrically stifled yawns and anecdote-ending sighs of disinterest any less annoying, or cruel to those who did not know her. I think now that's what attracted Dario to her, the idea that it was all a performance on her part, a way to mystify and intrigue. We broke up about a week before the three of us were to drive to Chicago for a concert. They ended up going by themselves, leaving in his Acura as friends and coming back from Chicago as lovers. That's how it happened. I felt a bit annoyed that it was she who told me about it and not him, since I saw him first and he acted as though nothing had happened on the trip. But then, and I know this is childish, I felt sort of good that he was the rebound, and at times I even thought and still sometimes think she got with him just to get back at me. See, there was really no intimacy between them, no heat in their interactions with each other, they were like brother and sister in public, and even though they dated for several years, I think it was just her dependency and his niceness that didn't allow either to finally end it. That didn't stop him from cheating on her; he's always been sort of a womanizer, a lover without memory, as the poets say. He spoke to me about these other girls very frankly—sometimes I even blushed at how explicit he was, like about this one waitress he knew I found attractive myself—but I felt proud, stupidly proud, that he confided in me, trusted me with his secrets. I should have told him to either stop the affairs or let Aida know. But I didn't. When they broke up, there were all kinds of rumors as to why they did, all of them nonsense. Aida and I are good friends again, as close as we were before *our* break up, but she has never talked to me about him, their relationship or why it ended, and I respect that. Most likely, once Dario got accepted into graduate school, he saw his way out and broke up with her. Their relationship probably ended as passionlessly as it begun. But there's more. Aida went to law school and there she met a guy. A couple of years later, they got married. Halfway through the festivities, Dario unexpectedly walked into the banquet hall in his finest suit and nonchalantly made his way to the table where his parents were sitting. I saw his mother cross herself at the sight of him. When I went over, I also saw he was high and already drunk, and he just kept on drinking. Barely able to stand as we lined up before the bride and groom, Dario gave Aida a rose with an exaggerated awkwardness and longing only a husband could miss. And as the band sat down for a pause, he yelled at them to keep playing, songs of joy and forgetting, yelled at the guests to clink their glasses together until their glasses broke, to overturn all the tables and set fire to anything white. A fine performance, I said as I hauled him into my car, because that's all it was, all it seemed to me. I understand you can sometimes do out of love the exact same thing you'd do out of hate, but how do you ruin someone's wedding out of a lack of these emotions, how do you beat up a defenseless kid and murder your girlfriend out of pure apathy?

Dina K.

He told me about his father, who struggled so much with the language that it embarrassed Dario overhearing him practice in his bedroom, pronouncing simple words over and over again, trying to annunciate. The pathos of a second tongue, Dario called it. He told me how his own tongue would grow fat, thickly un-American, and I remembered how he would sometimes stutter a word out in class. He told me his father was interned in the Omarska Camp, where he spent two years, starved, beaten, and humiliated, missing the funerals of both of his parents. His father, Dario told me, worked two jobs when they came to America and was never home, then quit both jobs and started driving a truck and still was never home. Dario spent more time with the fathers of his friends than with his own. He never spoke much of his mother. He told me he wrote on the rickety chair and table in the corner of the living room, often in his underwear. He let me read what he wrote while we rested after sex. All of his stories were about the war in one way or another. I tried to find myself and all the other women he'd known in the descriptions of his female characters. Was the orange heel mine? Were the feline cheekbones? To whom belonged the grape-plump lips? He told me what he missed most about St. Louis was the food, the dolmas his mother made, grape leaves as broad as the ear of an elephant, he said, spreading his arms wide and laughing. He also missed waking up to the chirping of sparrows and seeing them do tightrope skips on the black railing of the balcony. There were no sparrows where he lived in Arizona, only pigeons. He told me he stopped smoking weed and drank only a little, and that he didn't go to bars and clubs anymore because he could no longer stand it. Dario told me so many things while he kissed my back or caressed my thighs in the half-light of his bedroom. He told me about his childhood summers in St. Louis, the bright blue skies and the round burst of a fire hydrant, children playing in a fantasy of sun and water, and I couldn't tell if he was being sarcastic or not. Told me about what he did as a teen with his friends, how they sneered at speed limits and the dumb authority of stop signs as they drove drunk through empty streets at night, his mother waiting for him to come home. Told me how he now loved listening to our music, songs he hated when he was young, and then he would play me some Đorđe Balešević with such tender joy in his eyes. Told me about trying to translate into English the poems of Aleksa Šantić and Rilke, and then spoke about what he called the near elation of translation. Sometimes he laughed at his own jokes. He told me how he once beat up some American who complained about Dario and his friends speaking Bosnian at the bar during a soccer match, but when I tried to get him to tell me more, he didn't want to talk about it and was silent for a long time. Once he told me I was his best reader even though we never talked about his stories anymore after I read them. And once he told me that all Bosnian men live with the hurt of their fathers, then wrote it down in his notes. And once I got up the courage to ask if he based the mother character in the first story of his I read on his own mother and he said, Yes, no, only the stubbornness.

Haris H.

The air in the bar was already hazy blue with smoke by the time the players came out of the tunnel. The solitary billiard table in the back, on which my father had shown Dario and me how to play, was abandoned now, the sticks lying in an X on the synthetic green. Three waitresses darted back and forth. Franko was still behind the bar, waving at every new person that came through the door, nearly hitting the wineglasses that dangled above his head upside down like bats. Sliding into the horseshoe-shaped booth, I instantly wondered why I had come to spend my afternoon at a bar with bunch of people I didn't know or like anymore, if I ever did, watching a game I had outgrown, rooting for a team that didn't even exist when I was growing up. Dario was the one who played varsity in high school, not me. I remember asking him if he was any good back when we were deciding to try out for the team, and he said he wasn't really. Then he went on to play great and make the team and I did not. Was he being modest or was he lying? A lack of self-awareness or compassion? As I slid into my seat, I felt like I was talked into another try-out I'd for sure fail. And then the Dario I saw in public was not the same Dario I spoke to in my room, which annoyed me even more for having come. Public Dario was idle and trivial, hostile toward all attempts at sincerity, unconcerned with any questions that didn't have immediate answers, laughing at everything private Dario took seriously with a laugh slothful and bitter. It wasn't the weed or the alcohol, I don't think, because they were after all just simple coping mechanisms like his mother's timid faith. No, I don't think it was that at all, but just being in public, the discomfort of having to interact with large groups that brought it out in him, this exaggerated frivolousness and cynicism. Or maybe that too was just a way to cope, to endear himself to the crowd, even though he probably cared about them as little as I did. Like when the teams were lined up and the anthem started to play and the camera focused on each individual face as the Bosnian players mouthed the anthem, hand firmly on heart, and in the bar some tried to sing along with the same proud determination even though most of them seemed not to know the words, and I remember Dario just humming, then suddenly looking at me and smiling as though none of this mattered to him at all. Everybody was there, Aida, Vedad, Aldin, and the sisters, Lejla and Lana, who there's really nothing to say about other than that Dario had slept with both of them at one time or another, or even the same time if the rumors were true, though I doubt it. Everybody was drinking, Aldin and Vedad especially. And when Milan tried to leave the bar, it was one of them, and I've never been exactly sure which one, Aldin or Vedad, that yelled out in Bosnian, Take off that shirt, you fucking Serb.

Dina K.

How to describe to you the moment I recognized it was him in that grainy camera footage, the chill that ran up my spine, how hollowed out I felt, how devastated. I actually knew right away it was him, not because it made sense, not because it was something he would do, but because something inside of me recognized him instantly, that something that seemed scraped out of me as soon as I knew for sure it was him. I also knew the manhunt would end with his death, by his own hand, but that came from a different kind of insight, that had no love behind it. I have spent nights awake asking how could he, why did he, but *that* I don't know; I don't know why he told me all he did, why he thought I would understand, I don't know if it could have been me instead, or what finally made him snap? I told you before we began that I will not interpret him, only tell you what I have seen, heard, and felt during the time we were together, and that's what I have done. The last couple of months of our affair, or whatever you want to call it, I only saw him three times. The last time we were together I asked him where he'd been and he said he was in St. Louis taking care of some business. I thought he was joking, but it didn't feel like it, he was so cold and distant that day. Then he said he would go to Los Angeles with Laura, they were going to move in together, and so this was the last time he and I would be like this. Like this! I just nodded. Later I got a mass email inviting me to his thesis defense. I sat in the back row, he in the front with Laura next to him on the edge. She never once turned around to look behind her and so I never got to see anything but the back of her head. An older woman, frail, dark-haired, elegant in a long dress, sat on his other side and she kept looking behind her all the time, turning her head with an almost twitching motion. I remembered then how he once told me that he could always see, coming back from a night out, the light in their living room window, because his mother would stay up every night he was out waiting for him, and how the yellow light in the window became for him the very symbol of his mother's vigilance. There was no man beside her, no older version of Dario anywhere. Then Dario went up on stage, stood behind a podium and thanked everybody for coming. As soon as he began thanking his professors and fellow students, it became unbearable to listen to him. There was such bitterness and even hate behind the nice words he was forcing himself to say about them, as though he was desperately fighting off the urge to tell them what he really felt. When he thanked his mother it was with the same barely suppressed bitterness and rage. Then he turned toward the edge, looked at Laura, and it was as if all the bile he felt had come up into his throat and he couldn't speak. He didn't say anything, just swallowed, then turned back toward the center. She seemed heartbroken to me at that moment, and the gap Dario left when he got up, between her and the rest, seemed now an ocean and she was on her own sad little island, adrift. I know it sounds ridiculous, especially since I could only see the back of her head, but that's how I felt. She was hurt. And now she's dead. I felt the impulse to leave right then and there, but then he started reading and his voice changed and he seemed himself again, or the self I knew, and he read that story, one he must have written recently, he read it so tenderly and prayerlike that I couldn't move from my seat. I felt like I was under a spell, I was crying, but then he finished and his professors began asking him questions and he began answering them like he didn't care or like he hated being asked, and I left in the middle of it. Later that night, oh, I will be okay. Don't worry about me. Later that night I got an email from him, just for me, with the title of his story in the subject line, the attachment below and nothing else.

Haris H.

It may seem from an outsider's perspective, from an American's perspective, if he is knowledgeable about our history, as you clearly are, that coming into a predominantly Bosnian Muslim bar wearing a Serb jersey was an act of provocation, but I don't think anybody would have noticed Milan and his brother, who just wore a red T-shirt, had they not come in during half-time. But they did come in just then, but even so I don't think anybody really cared. Most of us knew Milan from high school, knew he was harmless, a quiet kid, a good student, who ate an apple every day during lunch. The only thing said at our table was about the fact he was born in Banja Luka, to Bosnian Serb parents granted, but still in the heart of Bosnia, and yet here he was wearing a Serb jersey. But that was more of an indication of Milan's confusion rather than his spite, said with the vehemence of an eye roll. They looked around for a table, talking to each other, and had to settle for one on a platform right next to the window, which made anybody sitting there, if viewed from the outside, resemble a mannequin in a storefront. That, I thought, was the end of it. The game was actually pretty good and a few times I found myself out of my seat and going toward the screen without realizing it. But the only goal came toward the end and the Serbs scored it. In the bar the buildup of nerves was released in a collective howl of such ardent grief, it was amazing. Dropping to their knees, clutching their heads, the very young imitating the old, everybody was cutting a tragic figure. Even Dario, who was half out of his seat, his head in his hands, stared at the screen with an expression frantic and empty with despair. He settled in his seat again, and this I remember vividly, picked up his beer, was about to bring it to his lips, then suddenly put it back down with a thud, the beer sloshing in the glass and spilling on the plastic-topped table. Look at them, he said calmly, just look at them, restrained like children at a funeral. And then the game ended and the brothers tried to make their way out and Vedad or Aldin called out to them, or actually just to Milan because his brother was already out, and then Dario got up and walked through the maze of tables as nonchalantly as he would years later at Aida's wedding, demanding of Milan in an even tone to give him the shirt. Give me that shirt, he said, walking toward him, and the plank of reason broke under the strain of human insanity. A push and Milan slammed against the door. He thrust forward but Dario pushed him back harder. Aldin and Vedad rushed toward the entrance. Milan's brother tried to reenter, but they blocked the door by pinning Milan against it. I felt the tension to move in my limbs but didn't leave my chair, and when I finally got up it was too late. Through the shifting foliage of the crowd amassing by the door, I momentarily saw Milan's face, turned to the side, eyes closed, lips rolled in, then saw it struck down by Dario's fist. Stop it all of you, Franko cried over the swell of voices, nearly climbing onto the bar, and I remember the plea only because it came in his pathetic broken English, as though our own language had lost the power to reach us. Dario tore away from the hands that eventually lifted him off the ground, he too yelling in English to let him go. He left through the back, Aida running after him. The brother came in and we all just stood there dumbfounded around the reclining bulk of Milan, whose shirt covered half his face, the neckhole torn, blood coming out his mouth. At that moment, and I swear this is true, I just wanted to grab Dario by the jaw with all five of my fingers, restrain him against a hard surface and make him look into my eyes as he explains to me just what the fuck is wrong with his mind.

Dina K.

The story he read at his defense and sent to me the same night begins with a description of a boy stealing figs from his neighbors' garden. Damir's his name and he's stealing the figs because he likes the neighbors' daughter, Jelena, a slender girl who spends most of her free time practicing the piano with her mother. Damir can hear the music from his backyard, Chopin and Liszt, teasing the fig thief's nerves. He is described as lanky and athletic, tall for his age, funny and daring and effortlessly normal in the company of others. As he gets older he smuggles blue jeans from Italy when he is supposed to be doing something else. He goes to Zagreb to study Economics, leaves Jelena but cannot forget her. He learns English, reads the Romantic poets when he is supposed to read Adam Smith, and thinks about her all the time. He adores the poetry of Keats and writes nothing. Instead of preparing for his exams, he spends summers with pretty German girls and beautiful Czechs wandering Croatian beaches, all in vain. He quits school after two years, coming back home an inspired failure. She has grown tall and even more beautiful and Damir tells her she's the reason he has come home. Her long, thin fingers play across his shoulders and over his back like a piano. They love each other with an angry and devouring love. They learn one another's insecurities and hurt each other with the truth. They fall into fits of competitive silence. They fight with intensity and a misguided devotion. It's 1992. Damir is conscripted into the army and leaves her. She writes to him but he never writes her back. She stops writing, too. When he returns suddenly, Damir is a changed man, out of love. His humor has become bitter, his daring nihilistic. He finds that he has deserted the army to see the only woman he ever loved get married to another man. He makes a fool of himself at the wedding, unloading a rifle into the air. He's Muslim and Jelena is Orthodox, and when war breaks out, the

Serb paramilitary, made up of his former friends and neighbors, her brother and cousins, kills him in his house as they overtake the village. Jelena mourns him in secret until the end of her life. His death is described in a direct and unsentimental way by the omniscient narrator. Damir doesn't defend himself because he has wasted all his bullets at a wedding. He doesn't even flinch as a bullet punctures his heart, tender as a fig.

Image, distortion, conflation—the knight move
of metaphor.
Ivan Borić

Writing is prayer.
Franz Kafka

We are alone and in love, suddenly and too late.[1]
Ivan Borić

Witness to a Prayer

This biography of sorts is the result of three meetings I had with Vesna Borić, the widow of Ivan Borić, perhaps the greatest prose stylist in Serbo-Croatian. A fellowship to Prague gave me the opportunity of arranging these interviews with Mrs. Borić, who has been living in Prague since she and her husband emigrated there from the former Yugoslavia in August of 1992, one month after the death of their only child, Mila. Mrs. Borić

---

1. These two quotes are from the last notebook Ivan Borić kept for his planned collection of stories, tentatively called *Basements and Other Museums*, and they perfectly emphasize his sense of aesthetics as well as his sense of pathos, the balance all great writers seem to possess between the cerebral and heartfelt. Sandwiched between them is the famous quote by Franz Kafka that inspired the title of this piece.

answered my questions to the fullest possible extent, even those that caused a new recognition of an old loss in her very large, very green eyes (so often borrowed by the late author and rented out to his female leads). For this I am most thankful. I have tried my best here to translate into a flowing narrative the information Mrs. Borić provided me about her husband; I have tried to give a detailed and accurate, albeit short, account of his life. If I have failed to make this incredible writer exist in the reader's mind, the fault lies solely with me. At one point during our last meeting, I was tempted to throw out the note cards in my square pocket and turn to Mrs. Borić and simply ask her to tell me everything about him, everything she knows and everything that's unknowable too.

One last note on the interviews that produced this small biography: I got lost trying to find our meeting place, a little café on Kaprova, as soon as I got out of the tram, and it felt as though it was my fate, that sly, grasping deity so often impersonated by the author, to follow in the footsteps of his protagonists, those wing-heeled travelers who find themselves blissfully lost in foreign surroundings, never pausing to wonder how they will return home, only to notice a copper inscription on a synagogue or the white lily scent in a city garden, or the dancing iridescence of raindrops against the pavement of some nameless seaside town.[2]

---

2. The last example is taken verbatim from page 16 of "Apropos Madeleine," my favorite short story from *Life Under Embankment Lights* (Svjetlost, Sarajevo, 1986). The first two examples are paraphrases, approximations of Borić's prose style. I have set out in this piece to deliberately copy Borić's style, his imagery and diction, his syntax and rhythm, his imagination and legerdemain, in an effort to provide a more vivid picture of his experience of the world (though compared to his singing prose, mine is only a hoarse whimper, a card trick to the parting of the sea). I believe, as Borić did himself,

1

Ivan Borić was born on April 21, 1955, in the Old Town of
Mostar,[3] the birthplace of many former poets. As a mature
artist, he would recall many parts of his happy childhood and
scatter them throughout his art: the L-shaped balcony of the
family house on Fejić, with its square of cramped shade and
the cellophane effect of reflected light in the lone window;
the dusky basement in which he once found a dead mouse, a
foretaste of his mortality; the blurred view of the toilet and
sink through the ribbed glass of the shower door, a foretaste of
his style; his mother, Enisa, blowing on a spoonful of bubbling
sauce in the tomato and mint haze of the kitchen; the thud
and flutter of books and typewriter paper, and sometimes just
Chopin, coming from behind the closed door of the study,
where his father, Miroslav, sat in a leather and oak armchair,[4]
at a mahogany desk as broad as a sarcophagus, revising by hand
his lecture on Hegel or Kierkegaard. It was the study, more than
any other place, that fascinated Ivan as a youth. (He was an
only child.) The dense shadows at either side of the bookcase,

that a writer's consciousness is reflected in his style, and in trying to capture
the way he wrote, I am trying to capture the way he thought, remembered,
and dreamed.

3. When, as a seventeen-year-old budding writer, I asked my father what
Yugoslav authors I should read, Ivan Borić was his only answer. Great writer
and from Mostar, my father said with pride. The obvious choices such as Ivo
Andrić and Meša Selimović did not attract me at the time with their robust
historical melodramas and soulful neurotics. I wanted something different,
more exhilarating and dreamlike, and I found it in Ivan Borić's work.

4. In *Oroz* (Svjetlost, Sarajevo, 1990), the novel's supposed hero, Vedran
Vidević, imagines his father, another professor, also sitting in such an
armchair, calling it "the emaciated throne of philosophy" (pg. 82). As in the
epigraph, all the translations in the footnotes are mine.

the blue glimmer of the ceiling fan's rotating blades, and, most intriguing of all, the blazing rungs of light reflected from the wooden window blinds, an abrupt ladder on the parquet floor.

Like many great writers of prose, Ivan started out as a poet. Yet from his first poem, written on *24 January, 1970* (he put a date in the bottom right-hand corner of each emergent poem, to give it a romantic authenticity), to his last, written on *10 May, 1973*, he never wrote anything with which he was completely satisfied, and looking back over this short period of verse he only appreciated it as a necessary step in his artistic progression, cherishing here and there a small pocket of brilliance and beauty: here, the slick thump of a leather soccer ball, there, a small girl's elegant tug at a limp sock.[5]

They would meet in Partizan Park, on leaf-dappled benches near statuesque pines, a bunch of student poets, Ivan's friends from the gymnasium, reading their lyrics to each other and the crickets. So many distant mountains! She was among them sometimes, a freshman, Marko Novak's sister, the silent participant in a loud circle, biting her thumbnail or peeling a translucent piece of skin from her upper lip. Ivan barely noticed her, only that she was tall, displaying in her movements that touching discomfort of young women not yet accustomed to their stature, and that there was a long albino scar on her left ankle, perhaps from a slip on beach rocks.

---

5. These snippets of his poetry, like any other facts of his life, exist only insofar as Mrs. Borić can recall them. Her feat of recollection in general, and her recitation of long-lost poems in particular, remind me of Dragan in "Apropos Madeleine" hearing his future wife, Diana, from the balcony below his, "humming to a melody from the radio, then to the memory of it" (pg. 3). It also reminds me somewhat dejectedly of Dragan's assertion toward the end of the story that "memory is the most unreliable of narrators" (pg.17). The story is partly set in Makarska, Croatia, where Ivan and Vesna Borić often vacationed.

Ivan had known Marko only for a while and they quickly lost touch when Ivan moved to Sarajevo to attend university, and he didn't think of Vesna at all, except that sometimes at night, during intense fits of insomnia, he saw her suddenly reflected against his inner lids, dressed in the thigh-length shorts and sleeveless shirt of her volleyball uniform, vivid, knee-high socks covering her scar. The image recurred throughout his years in Sarajevo, and one especially terrible night he finally tracked down its source, remembering how Marko had once come to pick him up with her in the backseat, how she sat in the middle of the seat quietly until they dropped her off at practice, slouching as much as her tall body would allow in the tight space and looking out of the left-hand window, her profile somber—how, as the car took a steep, slow curve, she turned slowly away from the window and met his gaze in the rearview mirror, her big green eyes infused at the moment with the infinite tenderness of human abstraction.

At the University of Sarajevo, Ivan studied his father's trade, though he spent most of his time writing short stories. In the middle of his second year, he dedicated himself totally to the double enchantment of reading and writing. Indeed, late at night, unable to sleep, his eyes open to the motionless shadows on the wall, the snoring of one roommate and the heavy breathing of the other an accompaniment to his fantasies, he imagined that this period of his life would one day be a significant chapter in his future biography.[6] His short stories,

6. Viktor H., the narrator of *A Eulogy for Viktor H.* (Svjetlost, Sarajevo, 1985), also spends nights awake thinking about his future biography and the man he has chosen to write it, "Ivan Borić," mocking in parenthesis "those poor, unenviable fellows, future biographers, always the last to know" (pg. 78). Like Vidević after him, Viktor H. suffers from "the ghostly vigil of insomnia," (pg. 121), a recurring motif, a ridge in the thumbprint of authorial presence.

so short on story, were often in the form of mock confessions and oblique autobiographies, interpretations on the notion of memoir. In them the reader can already find themes that would recur in his work such as the dual nature of man, the shared sphere of reality and dream, life's subtle beauty and its elegant lack of meaning. Through his prose style he gestured toward the dazzling slits in the mask of everyday life, those sublime hints at the harmony of existence, which a true artist feels like a running shiver down the spine, a leaping flame in the heart that illuminates the hollowness.[7] Ivan's reason for writing had always been an avid desire to describe the world; to impel and aid the reader to imagine a smile, a smell, the play of light at dawn, the voices in the street—all the small, overlooked miracles of life. Indulge in swarming, enthusiastic, narcissistic, veracious description. Embrace the caress and warmth of details. Imprison beauty in a padded sentence. This for him was the supreme pleasure of art. Let the scientist explain and the philosopher interpret—the artist must bear witness and describe.

Yet what a demeaning struggle it was, and what an intolerable bore, trying to answer the question of why he wrote, especially when he knew or sensed that the interlocutor thought writing a trifle, an adolescent hobby, that there was something ridiculous about a grown man playing quiet games with his noisy imagination. What further complicated his explanation

---

The character "Ivan Borić" will henceforth be written with quotation marks.

7. The faint literary criticism in this brief paragraph is my humble opinion of the thematic focus of Ivan Borić's fiction and the metaphysical implications of his style. Mrs. Borić's opinions are quite similar to mine, yet neither her nor my *interpretation* constitute a "truth" (a princely word that, like reality, must always be attended by its royal guard of quotes) of Ivan Borić's art, or Ivan Borić as an artist.

was that in conversation he invariably left one part of his reason unsaid—embarrassed by its seeming sentimentality, its daunting simplicity—which was a desire not only to reconstruct a torn down building, or resurrect a severed tree, but also to relieve the human dead of death and grant them immortality. The dear dead; the immortality of art. But how hopeless it was to relay this desire, the exquisite joy of it, with its ripple of transcendence and blasphemy—to say to an inquiring stranger that he, Ivan Borić, wrote to capture beauty and raise the dead.

At the University of Zagreb, where he obtained his doctorate, majoring in English Language and Literature, Ivan continued to write and publish short stories. But already by the end of the first year, despite his work appearing in prominent journals like *Gusle* and *Riječ*, he was hungering for the wide grazing range and thick concealing undergrowth of the novel. That summer, while at home in Mostar, he began to do the necessary research, filled notebooks[8] with promising scraps of imagery (the purest expression of the abstract bliss of observation), reread his favorite novels, studying in particular their sturdy, weatherproof structure, and tempted insomnia with hazy, half-blind fumbles for pen and paper to obsessively scribble something that in the sober morning became either completely unremarkable or else

---

8. Here are some of my favorites from his last notebook, which Mrs. Borić allowed me to borrow in Prague: "the dream of childhood from which the war woke her;" "all whispers are urgent, it is the whisper's way of being loud;" "Brodsky's cabin in Archangel, Russia;" "the ghostly oscillation of an abruptly deserted swing;" "equine beauty of Mostar's hills;" "her bruise the color of crushed figs;" "the flame fluttered like a bullfighter's cape;" "pelicans are only swans with venetian masks;" "Rilke, Lermontov, Paul Celan—what is inspiration but the whisper of ghosts?;" "the window frame reflected in his coffee;" "…by sleight of fate;" "golden lilies eavesdropped in the wind;" "in memory the rain always falls sideways;" "nothing is more ~~patient~~ impatient than the grave;" "a blood-soaked tissue is not a rose."

impossible to read. Such was the urgency of his muse, losing a
shoe as she ran to embrace him. He'd long had the idea of an
intelligent, ambitious man, Viktor H., a writer without talent,
who plans an act of terrorism in the streets of Sarajevo. Yet
Viktor H. is no revolutionary, nationalist, or religious zealot,
follows no ideologies, has no political beliefs whatsoever, and
does not bargain with God; a dangerously superfluous man, he
tries to achieve greatness and immortality through destruction
and death. He is caught easily, writes a "confession" from prison
to prove his sanity and repent, and then takes his denial of life
to its stoic conclusion by committing suicide days before his
trial. But there must be a doppelganger, a shade, Ivan thought,
coming through the tall doors of the humanities building, the
protagonist's childhood friend, perhaps, a true artist—though
the reality of the artist is as much in the limbo of quotation
marks as the reality of the terrorist—who is initially brought
along in the hope that he will write a posthumous book on
Viktor, a biography of the anti-hero. Ivan went up the broad
stairs, which an army could climb, turned left instead of right,
and picked up his pace like a man who feels the first ghostly
drop of rain on his forearm. (He was late for his first class as
Anton Kovačević's assistant.) What if the childhood friend
provides extensive annotations to Viktor's pseudo-confession,
an eccentric endnote commentary, as well as an intro and index?
Ivan liked that idea a lot. Furthermore—passing the inky blur of
the bulletin board and turning a corner—the childhood friend
should be called Ivan Borić. And what if[9]—he turned another

---

9. I know that in this passage the facts I've been given begin to grow wings,
but I feel it is important to evoke his innermost thoughts in order to make
him more vivid on the page, to create the intimacy and immediacy usually
missing from a secondhand account. See footnotes #2 and #5.

corner and bumped heavily into a girl coming the opposite way. The collision was severe; the poor girl sprawled on the ground like a starfish. He helped her up, went to fetch the book that had slid down the hall, clumsily kicked it even farther when he tried to pick it up, dropped it as he ran back, and then nearly dropped it again as he handed it to her. The hope of sneaking into class unnoticed had vanished; the only conciliation was the empty hall. The girl, mousy and black-spectacled, pressed the book to her chest, red-faced, her glasses knocked crooked, accepted his apology like she would a toad and scurried away. Ivan just stood there, and it took him a while to distinguish the laughter behind his back from that in his head. He turned, the way one turns in a dream, and there she was, gently and wickedly smiling.

With impromptu grace, Ivan bowed to his audience of one. From the debris of a shared past they tried to build a conversation until she bent her elbow to check her watch. He told her he'd walk her to her class, but she said they were standing right in front of it, causing him to make the long, wide-eyed face one makes when walking in on fate. Later on, when they were already dating, he overheard her relate the story of their meeting and put herself in the place of the gawky duckling he had accidentally trampled. He never called her out on it, for he must have known she'd plainly and shamelessly state that her version of events made for a better story. Indeed, her telling had a more daring touch of fate that gave the story a certain perfection. And perfection, of a kind, is the aspiration of all artifice.[10]

---

10. "Ivan Borić," after catching Viktor H. in a white lie, comments on the relationship between life and art, that "all writers merge memoir with fiction and fiction with memoir, creating fusion works, artful hybrids, swarthy centaurs and smiling mermaids. Truth is elusive and not adequate. Even life's most ingenious designs must be more perfectly shaped, even its best-

Neither of them had been punished for their tardiness that day because Anton Kovacević arrived even later, a habit of his along with the absentminded brush of pudgy fingers through thinning hair and the distracted tone of voice as he read his notes to *Mansfield Park* and *Bleak House* against the quick, cricketlike noise of scribbling pens. Ivan sat in the corner of the auditorium, facing the ascending rows of seats, trying not to be caught staring; Vesna sat in the second row, twelfth seat from the right. They began dating and went to the movies, got coffee and ice cream in those attractive side streets in the city—narrow rows of tables and chairs, shade umbrellas in full bloom—or sometimes just sat talking for hours on a bench in Republic Square, feeding the fat, high-breasted pigeons. They frequently stopped by the botanical garden, walking the pebbled paths, touching bark against their palms, and trying to read the scientific names of the flowers: Helleborus atrorubens, Adonis vernalis, Campanula poscharskyana, which was her favorite, a simple, star-shaped beauty, with arched lavender petals, vaguely tongue-like. Once, while circumventing a pond within the garden, he paused to write down in a small notebook she carried in her purse for him a description of water lilies. Then, with a sweep of his writing arm, a gesture that included the water lilies, the leaf-lined branches replicated in the pond, and the partition of conifers in the sun-shot distance, he told her this was what he meant when he talked about research.

Ivan was renting out a room by Maksimir Park during his time in Zagreb, and Vesna would often stay the night rather

patterned themes further enhanced by the pen. As an artist, I, too, bent the truth to fit my fiction. I invented a better truth, I told the poetic truth, I imagined, I lied. I lied about life and stole from it like from a favorite author. Like Viktor H., I plundered my life for all its silks, and out of these real silks I have spun my web of make-believe" (pg. 142).

than take the long tram ride back toward her dormitory near Jarun Lake. She thought he was too cramped in this room, the back of the chair bumping into the footboard of the bed, but he enjoyed the solitude it afforded him, being far away from the bustle, clamor, and kitsch of the dorms. His insomnia was less powerful when she shared his bed, backing into him, his heart beating against her spine as they slept. He drank her in, her breathing, moving, olive-bright skin, the faint chestnut smell of her hollows, the languorous bends of her long body. The transparent blue vein that ran the inner length of her left thigh was like a cousin of the white scar across her ankle. Volleyball injury, she told him, surprised that he kissed her there. The tip of her nose was always a little cold and damp, no matter how well he covered her in the middle of night when she slipped out of the blanket. He was absolutely entranced by the sleek upward curve of her big toes. But there was nothing as poignant about her body as some random reminder of its absence: the scratch mark of her eyeliner against the white of a pillow, the smell of her on the sheets, a long mirror-reflected strand of her black hair sticking to his chest.

In May of 1981, Ivan and Vesna married. After a summer spent back in Mostar, including a brief honeymoon on the Black Sea coast,[11] they returned to Zagreb for Vesna to continue her

11. Ivan and Vesna Borić shared a love of travel, among other things. The second time we met, Mrs. Borić surprised me with photographs of their trips. She sitting in a gondola with Mila in her lap, behind her shoulder the gondolier's dark glossy waistband, Ivan Borić reflected in miniature in her sunglasses, a flash at his heart; Mila bowing to smell a red rose in the former Royal Garden in Athens, the shadow of the photographer's bent elbow visible on the white gravel; Ivan Borić leaning over the stone parapet of the Charles Bridge the first time they visited Prague, lost in thought, or pretending to be for the camera; the entire family in front of the blurred columns of a wealthy Armenian merchant's house in Plovdiv, taken by a stranger with

studies and Ivan to start writing his dissertation, *God and the Novel: A Problem of Omniscience*. The baby was born at the end of October, a healthy girl, weighing five kilograms, named Mila. Ivan defended his dissertation the upcoming September; a year later Vesna passed her final exams. They went back to Mostar, where Ivan got a job teaching at the same gymnasium he himself had attended. They moved into his parents' house, living in the large guestroom across from the study that Ivan now shared with his father.

A Eulogy for Viktor H. was released by Svjetlost on July 26, 1985 and received a rather lukewarm reception from the critics (Ivan did not care to read reviews of his work, so Vesna read them for him), both in independent journals like *Petla* and *Gusla* as well as state-sponsored ones like *Borba* and *Brotherhood and Unity*, the latter expected since Ivan was not part and refused to join the Yugoslav Communist Party, but the former a bitter surprise despite Ivan's external protestation of complete indifference. Only in *Riječ* was the novel unequivocally praised; in those pages Danilo Kiš, one of a very few Yugoslav writers Ivan considered a contemporary, proclaimed the novel a masterpiece, calling its author "a verbal acrobat in clown's garb." When Ivan's first collection of short stories, *Life Under Embankment Lights*, came out on February 6, 1986, it did so to much more favorable reviews.

Immediately after the release of his short story collection, Ivan Borić started work on his second novel.[12] He was writing

---

trembling hands. None of the photos were from the war or after. There are a few photographs, Mrs. Borić said, but Ivan always has his eyes closed in them like a sleepwalker.

12. *Oroz* follows my namesake's move into the house of Franz Heinrich, a Yugoslav-born German, a Nazi sympathizer and aesthete, who owns a cemetery in the mythical town of Oroz. (The novel is set on the eve of

in the study one morning when Mila twinkled in through the open door. Ivan laid down his pen. She swung from the arm of his chair, leaning away on her heels, arms outstretched, and then leaning back in and pushing up on the balls of her bare feet, a question in her upturned green eyes. Yes, he said, and moved to the sofa by the door, opposite the bookcase. With a foal-like bounce to her step, she ran out of the room to get her notebook. This was all in keeping with the reassuring rhythm[13] of their lives: she coming in on the tips of her long toes to ask a question and the aching pleasure of his new novel fading

---

World War II, when the newfound republic of Yugoslavia disintegrated from internal and external pressures.) Franz has a daughter, Mila, and Vidević is her new tutor. These are the main characters, but the novel's true focus, its heart and soul, is its narrator/author, a vibrant and verbose spirit that colors the book. The poignancy of the novel comes from the narrator/author trying desperately to connect with the characters he is writing about, to reach them through his imagination, for their actions, or rather the actions of their similar-minded real-life counterparts, will have an impact on the his life later on. (The novel was released in October of 1990, less than a year before the second and final break up of Yugoslavia.) The narrator/author fails and his failure becomes part of the novel he is writing. The realization of his failure corresponds with Nazi Germany's invasion of Yugoslavia: the two worlds of the novel merge in their destruction. Rather than reading *Oroz* as a parody of transcendence, as some critics have done, I think it should be read as a transcendent parody.

13. A scene between Heinrich and Vidević in the former's garden is interrupted by Mila riding by on a bike, then further interrupted by the narrator/author asking rhetorically if anyone has, "in a poem maybe, captured that enduring father and daughter scene, the daughter paddling swiftly, jittery on the bike, the patient father trotting alongside, holding the edge of the handlebar and the rear of the seat, the daughter relaxing a little, softening the tight grip on the bars as she achieves a certain reassuring rhythm, confident, delighted, she turns her head bravely to share with her father this triumph, but there is no father, he is a long way down the street, a gesturing blur, yelling just go on, you are doing good, but all is lost, the daughter fumbles and the bike teeters and they both crash, she scrapes her knee, suspends bike-riding for a month" (pg. 124).

instantly before the slit shadows of her dimples. Mila came back and sat next to him. He opened the notebook on his lap and marveled at the drawings of dresses, skirts, blouses, hats, and swimsuits. She nudged into him, explaining the sketches over the blue-edged drone of the ceiling fan, and pointing an ink-stained little finger at what to pay attention to. Ivan knew he loved her for selfish reasons, yet he also knew he loved her more than he loved himself. The blinds were up. The pages rustled and lisped. Her reddish-brown hair gleamed like an apple in a sunbeam. A square of light quivered on the hardwood, seeming about to lift itself into the third dimension at any moment.

2

It was seven in the morning and Ivan was awake, watching a game of chess between the light and shadow in his room until dawn erased the chessboard. His temporary room. Everything was temporary now. He would lie in bed pretending to be asleep for Vesna's benefit, knowing she did the same. At one point in the night he had seen her winding silhouette against the window, sitting on the sill, her knee raised, one foot resting on the edge of a dark bulky thing. She was asleep now, he could tell by the indelible rhythm of her respiration. He slid out of bed quietly and got ready for his walk. While he washed and shaved, Prague was being staged outside, the buildings and church towers propped up, the Czech sky molded like papier-mâché, the air brushed with the sharp, elusive shimmer of reality.

Back in the bedroom, Ivan disentangled the blanket twisted around Vesna's legs and covered her up to her throat. There was still the undercurrent of chestnuts, but now her skin, her curves and hollows, smelled predominantly of bread. The soft white part, not the orange crust. He stood before the mirror, buttoning his long coat, a little stunned, a little baffled to be here in Marko's apartment on Benediktska Street. The mirror proved only the existence of his reflection. He locked the front door, went down the stairs and out into the deceptive sunlight of a September morning, the collar of his coat turned up. There was a light wind in the cobbled alleys; sparrows and pigeons called from telegraph line to telegraph line. The air was damp from last night's rain, ripe-smelling. The sun in the shop windows made them opaque. He took Dlouha all the way to the Old Town Square, his fists like two stones in his pockets, his steps heavy and imprecise, his body drunk with cold. He remembered the square stack of firewood in the backyard of his parents' house in Mostar, how the logs had turned dark blue in the rain. He remembered Mila walking a few steps ahead of him toward the beach in Makarska, walking barefoot over pebbles and pine needles, the white hairs on her narrow brown back. He hoarded this image against some unimaginable winter. Of the five benches that encircled a large tree on an intersection island, only one was occupied. An old man in a flat cap was reading a newspaper while his dog smelled the leaves on the ground, the dog's hanging tongue as pink as the inside of a watermelon. Ivan passed them, remembering the dark-blue logs in their square stack, the sunburned, leaf-dappled shoulders of his daughter. Behind him, the old man sneezed, or the dog barked, and in front of him Mila walked long-legged in bathing shorts, crossing the square, past the fountain in the center, past men in overalls setting up a stage, past the wedge of peach light between two buildings, past the carriages with their

black and white horses, past St. Nicholas Church and back into
the dream-lit maze of narrow and never-ending streets.

Ivan had written in his notebook, during the train ride
from Zagreb to Prague, that for a man on the brink of a cliff,
everything is peripheral but the abyss. This is how he felt on his
walks through Prague: Everything melted together, the baroque
facades and the bottle green puddles in which they were
reflected, the beggars and the sidewalk they bowed against. He
knew he was on Kaprova because he had passed their café, and
he knew that Kaprova would lead him to the Vltava River. The
notebook, where was it now? He had no energy to write, no
desire. His muse had deserted him, dragging a suitcase behind
her like a sled. At night he did not think about writing anymore.
The firewood gleamed in the sun after the rain had turned the
logs dark blue, untouched. What had he been doing in the study
when he heard the explosion? Where had he been in relation
to the sound? It didn't matter; the sound had been everywhere
and he nowhere where he could have made a difference. But
he still needed to chart his location at the moment of impact.
Her skin was tight from the sun, her pale lashes even paler. He
followed her to the beach, leaf-shaped shadows sliding across
her shoulders and rushing down her back.

The small garden across from the Rudolfinum was empty. He
shielded his eyes to look up at Dvorak and then began to round
the base of the statue for a better angle of his face. Mila could
not fully understand that each calm in the bombing did not
mean an end to the war and so seemed always as unprepared
for the next round as she was for the one that had come before
it. Thunder, he had said to make her stop crying, even though it
was much larger than thunder. It would end soon, he had said,

even though it would never end, because endings were the very thing she misunderstood. He felt a sudden spasm in his chest and throat and sat down on a nearby bench. Regret had a way of startling him. He breathed in and out, slowly, conscious of the effort. A woman bent over him and Ivan gave her a hand gesture of reassurance, vague with exhaustion. He was fine, he told her, in his own language. She patted him on the back and left. He watched her disappear behind a building and his eyes closed almost without his knowing.

He watched Mila sleep in the candlelight. He watched her chest fall and rise among the wavering shadows in the basement.

Ivan sat trembling on the bench; the harder he tried to control it the more he trembled. The edges of his world began to blur, but he shook it off. Sparrows looked for food in the shadow of a dead man's statue. Flecks of sunlight caught in the shrub leaves. The buttons of Ivan's coat heaved. No description could have captured the unreality of that moment: the bright hard burst of sound that had been everywhere as he was nowhere, the humid rubber smell of the alley, the drying firewood in the backyard, gleaming in the sun. She held a purple pinecone in her hands like a baby bird, raising her elbows to show him. Each night he lay awake measuring his own complicity. He could not find himself at that moment, even in the study he was not there. Each night he lay awake, his eyes open, his eyes closed, watching her sleep.

There was pain in his legs as he got up from the bench, pain and a lightness—the dreaming limbs of a hanged man. Sunlight flickered in the shrubs while sparrows chirped at the periphery. Everything buzzed with the insatiable amber of fall. Everything rustled and breathed. Mila would be eleven soon. Mila would never be eleven.

The river was his compass. He walked alongside it to the Charles Bridge. Halfway across the bridge, he stopped to look down at the water. He had fed the logs into the fireplace when the electricity had gone out, and he remembered how the flames climbed but never reached. The smell of rubber, warm as a mouth, and apricot-colored clouds through moon-thin smoke. He flowed seamlessly into that moment from one unremembered. It was colder on the bridge and he could hear more clearly the scarf-muffled voices of the wind. A black-headed gull slanted toward the water. A girl rubbed the bronze plaque on a haloed statue, rising on her tiptoes. Some saint drowned in this river. He heard the wind without listening to it. His arms folded on the stone parapet, Ivan yawned at the water, weathering the first dull sting of tiredness. The water was yellowish-green where the sun hit it, violet and obliquely silver where the shadow of the bridge reached. He heard her voice like a bell whose vibration was still felt even when the sound had ceased. The spires of the east tower rippled in the water. There were only a few vendors on the bridge, but no musicians, and no artists painting portraits that made one's face look like it would reflected in a spoon. He imagined her heart compressing and expanding like shadows in the basement used to do when they passed the candle around from one to another. Her elbows rose to show him a purple pinecone, a flat pebble, a grasshopper in its green armor. He remembered the large red-orange fire, the black column of smoke, thinning out into silver as it rose, the clouds pierced by the sun, colors mixing, blurring, rushing. He did not understand endings either, not after her end, knew them only from books, where nothing really ended. Death and then what? Ivan did not believe in forewords or afterworlds. He did not believe in a God he could not imagine and refused to believe in a God he could. He did not believe in anything that could give him hope except his writing. But he could not write.

Last night he had opened the window of their temporary room on the third floor and stuck his head out. There were no mountains in the distance; only the crickets were familiar, night's EKG. Death and then what? A long, dark, cricketless silence. Ivan leaned his head out more, felt the rain on his scalp and forehead, thought about letting himself fall with the rain. He could not sleep and he could not write. He felt nothing down his spine but fear and regret, and in his heart he was aware only of the night's powerful refusal to yield anything to him.

Mila had been killed by a fragment from a mortar shell that had hit their neighbors' garage as she played with the neighbors' son. Never go outside without my permission, Ivan had told her. From the L-shaped balcony he had seen the army move on the hill. Now he focused on the brassy glare of the sun in the river. Never go outside. Fragment in the chest. Without my permission. Never go. The window of the room in which he forgot himself had been sheathed in plastic. This he remembered, the popping sound the plastic made in the wind. Then the quick blind thack-thack-thack of rifle fire. Then a deep bursting hardness. He did not understand it, the sudden violence of circumstance. Or fate, which he pretended to know the way the neighbors' boy, a sheet around his neck tied in a rabbit-ear knot, pretended. A cobblestone alley separated the garage from their backyard, where the logs gleamed dark blue in the sun after the rain. He remembered the fire in the alley where the children had played climbing into silver but never reaching the gold of the sky. He had held her in his arms bloodied and limp, and the memory of holding her was as feverish and vivid and stubbornly unreal as a dream. He remembered the white hairs on her hard brown back, the blue over her shoulder when they reached the beach. Mila walked into the water slowly, knees bent, back crooked, hands gliding over invisible furniture. He thought about it every night, how easy it would be. She hugged herself, hunching her shoulders, turned her head toward him, made her green eyes big and exaggerated her shiver. Vesna would be the widow of a great love, if not a great man. Something so touching about tall girls. The water up to her waist, Mila began to turn her body, painful and slow, then threw her narrow back against an oncoming wave, her hard narrow back into the wave. All he needed to do was raise his body over the parapet. On the tips of her toes, a bobbing head, with glints of brown shoulder in the blue, she called out for him to come in. It would be that easy. The waves were as sad and inarticulate as the wind. He felt a dark calm beneath the leaden river, the downward tug of a strong inner current. In the water, he picked Mila up shivering in his arms.

The edges of Ivan's world blurred again. Her alert shoulder blades, her small yellow-knuckled fist holding onto something dear, her dimples when she smiled, it was all gone with her and she would not return. Ivan felt like a child at the realization that she would not. He looked at the tower in the water, the wrinkled spires. Mila was no longer in the range of his vision, but he could still hear the echo of her voice. The swans in the river swelled and dissolved. The river burned. She was no longer but he could still.

Instead of taking the stairway off the Charles Bridge onto Kampa Island, as had become his habit, Ivan went back east on the bridge and then walked farther along the river. Feeling tired again, his legs aching, all he wanted was to lie down on damp familiar grass, but he knew his sleep would be brittle, full of the emblematic dreams he did not believe in as a young man. He unbuttoned the top buttons of his coat, took Narodni toward home. The sidewalk filled with the smells of the fast-food places he was passing, fleeting voices, the oblique coos of pigeons. The sky was pale and blue, like wet paper. There was a beggar in front of the stairs to the National Theater, genuflecting severely, his hands cupped above his bowed head. Ivan dumped change into his mute palms without looking at him and crossed the street. From the chair, he had been reading to her his latest chapter, Vesna sitting in bed with the sheets tousled around her waist, a swan in repose. She was staring out of the window at a large evergreen bloated by the falling rain, a tinge of melancholy to the loose shape of her open mouth. He stopped reading abruptly and it took her a while to notice. He sat down on her side of the bed, looked where she was looking. Taking his hands into hers, Vesna said what she had to say. Ivan would be a father. He stopped in the middle of the sidewalk to listen to a live piano from the inside of a café. His eyes closed almost without him noticing and his world shrunk down to sound. Tonight he would go to sleep and never awake again, but now he stood in front of a café, listening to the calm tremor of a live piano. She stared at a tree swollen with rain through large green daydreaming eyes.

Here is where I will leave him, walking toward Republic Square, making his way home. I imagine him nostalgic, thinking about the shy soaring quality of Chopin and the thick piercing smell of mint. I imagine him going back again to that day in Zagreb. Vesna is asleep now. He is happy and fearful. Her breath is shallow. The rain is dark and it gleams. I imagine him walking the cobbled streets through crowds of tourists, past the fleet-footed clatter of plates and the broken arias of maître d's, trying in his mind to pin down the perfect image of her. This is the last gift I make to him: Mila rising from the basement floor, her shadow rising with her and spilling over the ceiling like ink; Mila on a swing, Mila on a bike; little Mila asleep on the sofa in the study, wind through the open window blowing on her long curling toes; Mila bowing her head to smell a red rose, the pale, whispery hairs on her curved, slender, almost touchable nape.

I have written only for seven years, but I know that if I write for another seventy, my reasons for doing so would not change—like Ivan Borić, I would still be trying to capture beauty and raise the dead.

The Poet from Mostar

The checkpoint is on Rude Hrozničeka, between the building I grew up in and the one I occupy now as a soldier. Behind my former building the land runs down to the Neretva River, green, transparent water sloshing against blue and gray rocks. The Serbs destroyed the nearest bridge a year ago; a small dam formed from the debris where the river curves narrowly. I walk around my old neighborhood in a soldier's uniform, jungle-colored, tight around the shoulders, and boots in whose black I can never see my reflection. Our headquarters are in a couple of third floor apartments (#9 and #10) whose prior occupants left when war broke out a second time. There are birds on the useless telephone wires and children below in the yard of my former building. The gap echoes and glares. The birds are sparrows. The barefoot girls, in the shade of a skinny linden, clap their hands and sing an old rhyme, while the perspiring boys, heads bowed, rummage in the overgrown grass, their pockets bulging with bullet shells. People in the neighborhood recall when a Jeep full of drunk Serb paramilitary drove over the bridge that wasn't there, the nothingness that stretches from one side to the other, and crashed into the rocks and debris. At night all one can see is the moving darkness of the water.

All we shoot are birds, Mario says. He says it all the time. He falls on his knees in front of the open window, grabs his rifle and puts it into position. He closes his left eye and, slitting the right, lets his finger slide up and down the curve of the trigger. Even when I can't see them, I hear the cling clang of the shells in their pockets and know where they are. Leaning out of windows, their mothers constantly check on them, shouting instructions in bright, exhausted voices. Mario was one of the young men who dived every summer from the crowded Old Bridge into the cold water below. Sometimes he shouts threats down on the street at Prof. Abdić, who walks from his building to the checkpoint and back in a dirty shirt and sweatpants, his hands clasped behind him, one shoulder held higher than the other. Imbedded in my mind with the bridge itself is the straight, stoic form of those bodies, startlingly balanced in mid-air, plunging into the green transparency of the river and producing a sharp, ripping sound on entry. You're in the crosshairs, Emir, Mario yells from the pedestal of our third floor window, and Prof. Abdić waves meekly at the jokes of his former student, his other hand shielding his eyes from the sun. Death is instant, and what's left of the sparrow is only a kaleidoscopic puff of feathers.

This is Mostar, a place the children in the yard have heard called home by the same mouths that unashamedly call it hell. Prof. Abdić walks the allowed length of street he grew up and lived his entire life on, reciting poetry to himself like a madman. Before the war, he was a professor of Russian Literature at the University of Mostar, one of the four professors who for years gathered each Friday in our living room to play cards. I remember a room filled with blue cigarette smoke and the bitter whiff of plum brandy; the strange harmony that existed between the voices and the night, the former growing louder as the latter grew darker; I remember the rolled-up sleeves and undone top buttons, the black chips shining in the center of the table. I watch them play, unfolding my chair in front of my old building and acquiring a full view of the oval yard, consisting of a grassless patch of pebbles in the center where the children congregate shoulder to shoulder before a game of dodgeball, facing Sanel, who holds a blue rubber ball in his hands. Sanel is the oldest—he is thirteen—and tallest of them all, dark-haired and in denim overalls. Tina, the captain of the opposing team, is long-legged, pony-tailed, and sleepy-eyed. I remember my own childhood and the games we played, and I think to myself that growing up during war is the most unnatural thing in the world.

The front is three kilometers from our checkpoint; we get almost no direct fire and there is nothing to do. The smell across the river is ash; the sound, man-made thunder. When the war came to Mostar in the spring of '92, my family and I, after spending almost a month in basement after basement, escaped to Croatia, an uneventful journey, half of which I spent with my head between my knees. The Serbian siege of Mostar ended in June and we returned home in early August. But there was no home. There was the caved-in roof, the blackened apartments, the crumbling staircase, and the wonder of why the Serbs chose to bomb our building, but leave untouched the one connected to it. It was to Rodoč then, to my grandparents' house, where we lived out the uneasy peace. Cafés reopened amongst the rubble and, dutifully, people came to drink. A halfhearted reconstruction of the city began. From time to time, the Serbs lobbed a bomb from the mountains to remind us of their close proximity. Then, in May of '93, the new war started (within the still-ongoing war north and east of us) between the Bosnian Catholics and Bosnian Muslims, ending the increasingly sinister peace in Mostar.

Mr. Abdić writes poems in his empty apartment; sometimes during his evening walks, he reads them aloud to me, his most perceptive student in peacetime, his only student now. Some are about the sparrows on the useless telephone wires; others are about the boys hunting for bullet shells, their pockets singing. By the end of the first week of the new war, most of the male Muslim population on the west side was either deported to the east, with their families, or detained, alone, in Heliodrom, the prison camp in Rodoč that was previously a military airport. In rare cases, like a visit from the Red Cross, men are allowed to temporarily leave the camp and go home. Such a privilege was given to Prof. Abdić, because of his chronic back pain and connections within the camp. His wife and two daughters are in Germany. They fled before the Serb invasion; he came back alone during the short peace—which lasted just long enough to get his hopes up, he says—and was arrested when the new war started. Most of his poems are about the past: two lovers illuminated by the milky glow of a lamp on Lučki Bridge; an impromptu family picnic on the pebbled bank of the Neretva; an aproned baker on Fejić passing loaf after loaf to a blue-uniformed delivery man. I tell him I hear in his poems the moan of a sidewalk accordion and the ragged chorus of voices in Old Town cafés. I don't ask him why he returned because it's a stupid question and he expects better of his best student.

In the bedroom of #10 the windows are always open. Bottles of beer and homemade plum brandy, cans of soda and old newspapers are scattered all over the room. The wind sweeps up crumbs of food and sends them across the parquet, but it can't clear out the damp, acidic smell of sweat that hangs in the air. Graffiti covers one side of the wall, the others punctured with bullet holes. Occasionally, a cockroach crawls up and down the floor. It's the regret with which Mario says it that irritates me. He is on his knees, his left eye closed. Led Zeppelin's "Whole Lotta Love" jerks out of the radio he has brought from home, blending with the howl and wail of the children outside, drowning out the distant gunfire. I have never fired a shot, except in the air. His finger stops moving; a cigarette, unlit, dangles from the corner of his mouth. Sometimes I want to pummel him with all my strength, beat him into an awareness of suffering beyond his own. But then I think of what will happen if he fights back. Or worse, if he doesn't? The mess and the music gives the place a dorm room atmosphere, and I often imagine we are students freely indulging in this lifestyle rather than soldiers confined to it by war. We are twenty.

Don't shoot, Mario, I say. There are children out there. Prof. Abdić says that the nature of memory and time is like the nature of darkness and water and I don't quite know what he means. I met Mario in Rodoč, where I spent my weekends as a child and where he was born, and where our games consisted of chasing frenzied chickens and tormenting a chained goat. Once school started, we progressed to more ordinary games like dodgeball and soccer. Mario takes out the Makarov pistol he bought in Bulgaria before the war; he points it at the side of his head. He is in his undershirt, cargos, and boots, forgetful of past and present. The sweat shows underneath his armpits. The sky is dark and enormous, and after the laughter hushes and the clinking of bottles stops, the only sound comes from the mad concord of the crickets around us. Children move invisible in the night, real and imagined, their eyes bright and feral in the dark. Prof. Abdić carries photographs on him at all times, inside the waistband of his sweatpants: one of himself and his wife, snowflakes melting on their black coats, one each of his two daughters, and one of a crowd of Velež fans running onto the field to celebrate the cup win in 1981—a man has both feet off the ground at the moment the snapshot is taken, seeming to levitate. The past, Prof. Abdić likes to say, is a world of echoes and half-forgotten songs.

I remember a blue-eyed boy with long blond locks, a boy who got carrot-red freckles in the summer, a boy who, following the very first day of school, ran after the teacher, pulling on his jacket, to ask him if we needed to come back tomorrow. In one of his poems Prof. Abdić compares the destruction of the Old Bridge to an angered child tearing up the Mother's Day card he had so carefully crafted because he desired, in his malicious rashness, to inflict the most immediate pain. But that's just metaphor. Prof. Abdić's eyes are spinach green and he's as short as Pushkin. In sweet grimy adolescence, when I began to write poetry, Mario took up the guitar, each envious of the other's limited talent. For hours everyday he strummed on that acoustic guitar of his, while I intermittently sang. Or we'd both be singing along to Western songs on the radio. In the evenings we went out, always together, watching movies in the overcrowded cinema in the city with friends whose ethnicity and religion seemed completely unimportant. It will all come back to us one day, Prof. Abdić says, and then we will stand in front of each other cleansed and ashamed. His poem ends when Ottoman sultan Suleiman the Magnificent, whose image I remember from a painting in which he is depicted in profile, wearing a black shawl and an outsized white turban, commissions the building of the bridge.

Mario, mumbling to himself, lays the Makarov on the ground and leans back in the folding chair. He complains loudly of a headache because he is drunk. The light of the lamppost shines off his shaved head, and I feel betrayed by the sight of it. He smiles a wicked smile but its wickedness is halfhearted. Do you hear me? I say. Don't shoot. He is silent. Are you listening? I come closer. Under the strain of their shared fatherlessness, Prof. Abdić intones, gesturing with one hand, the other holding the paper, though he does not read off it. Shaved and gaunt, he looks older than he is, with dark-colored pouches under his green eyes. The perspiring boys hop from hot concrete onto cool grass, hunting for bullet shells. But in an instance their task is forgotten, when the white tank slinks closer, slowly, like an armored cloud. We give the UNPROFOR soldiers a hard time at the checkpoint. Smurfs, we call them, though we know they can destroy us instantly. But they won't. Blue and white are not colors of war, Smurfs, Mario yells as they pass in their wheeled tanks. We are as much observers as they are, but this is our country and we don't pretend to be able to will the war out of existence.

"How useless this is. Being a soldier, I mean."

"Because there's nothing to do?"

"Because it's just useless. Bombing our own city. You can't cross the Neretva, can't go to the other side. But that's Old Town. That's where all the good restaurants are."

"Would you prefer if the entire city was bombed?"

"Yes. I mean no. No because I live here. I don't know. All I know, all I have ever known with any certainty, is that I don't want to kill or to die."

"So that's your point. You're a coward."

This conversation only happens in my head and even there I can't make him understand. It's a lack of imagination, Prof. Abdić would say.

Prof. Abdić says he began writing poetry at fifteen, when it became impossible not to. His early poems were terrible, contrived and quickly abandoned, barely worth the cheek of the girls they were dedicated to. There were many, he says. As a student at the University of Mostar, where he would later teach, he started writing political poems and imagined stopping tanks with his pen, sparking peaceful revolutions, imagined his poetry being recited in crowded city squares by zealous youths, hungry and betrayed. But there was no spark and no fire, no knock on the door by the authorities, no condemnation or medal. My country didn't need my poetry, he says, or my silence. Mario picks the Makarov back up from the ground and points it at Robert, who has a screwdriver in his hand. The drunken cheering begins again and Robert dares him to do it. Mario's eyes are red; he says the gun is not loaded; he leans back in the chair, his stomach lowering and rising as if from great exertion. Someone has set a tire aflame; the orange-and-white-paneled barricades gleam in the bonfire. Sweat runs down Robert's neck and he groans under a sky enormous and dark, charged with our madness and fire. There is a military van in the yard and a yellow Jugo missing a tire. Once the laughter dies down, there is only the sound of the blinking crickets. Through the thin envelope I can read the last lines of Prof. Abdić's letter to his wife, which I send for him: I'm as unthinking and unfeeling as a stone. I have only enough for these letters. Breaking up parts of what I have written here into stanzas might yield a poem. Not a good one, but a familiar one, and may be of some comfort to you. Love, Emir.

Out of the bedroom of #10, "Gimme Shelter" can be heard, above us the chirping of sparrows, and behind us the pop of an occasional explosion. On a manhole in the yard of my old building, bullet shells, lined up in ascending order, glint in the sunlight. Tina walks an alley looking for her vanilla pudding among the leftover candies the UNPROFOR soldiers have distributed. She stops suddenly, only to rub her foot against her calve. Prof. Abdić and I walk up and down the street we grew up on, talking of literature, and the soldiers working on the lights of one of the barricades call "Muslim lover" and "dead man walking" after us. I have taught my daughters, Prof. Abdić says, to be blind to religious differences, to consider themselves the only ideal ethnicity, a Yugoslav, and to follow the ethics, the rainbow-bright ethics, of humanism. Should I regret now doing what's right? And how can you, the son of a Catholic man who never practiced and a Muslim woman who didn't either but couldn't just forget where she came from, how, forced to wear the uniform of the Croatian Defense Council, how can *you* display with any genuine inner passion the outer appearance of a Catholic and a Croat, or show any real desire for the destruction of a city you love and a people you never hated? When he speaks like that I wonder if the only difference between my view of the war and Mario's is a Muslim mother. If my anger is only disappointment? If you can right someone whom you have already forgiven? Tina is offered other candies but refuses. She sits down cross-legged in the pebbled clearing of the yard and throws her arm across her shoulder to scratch her back. We walk up and down the street, talking of *War and Peace, Crime and Punishment, Dead Souls.*

I come closer. "Mario, don't shoot" I say, and kick the rifle off-target with my foot, tipping him over like a tower.

"What's the matter with you? I wasn't going to shoot," he says, ascending slowly, in stages, like an illustration of an evolving man we saw in books from school.

"I bet you weren't going to shoot."

"If I said I won't then I won't, and if I want to shoot then I will."

"Why are you being an idiot?"

"They're just fucking birds."

"What did they ever do to you?"

From my folding chair I watch the children in the center of the yard, one half-standing behind Tina, the other half-behind Sanel, who flips a coin in the air, catches it in his right hand, brings it down on his left, and rejoices after slowly revealing which side it is, number or flame on the old Yugoslav dinar (slowly, as if extra time would have transformed it if it wasn't in his favor). Then I hear Tina shout and she begins running down the street. The children spring magically to attention and follow after her. Turning into a side street, the tank stops and is surrounded. They bang on the armor, producing a dull, tinkling sound, until a helmeted head pops out of the hatch. The young man, a boy, really, looks at the crowd assembled before him and starts throwing candy with a strangely flamboyant flair, like he's on top of a float in a parade. The little beggars push and shove each other, frantically untucking their shirts to use them as pouches. Only Tina refuses to push and shove as she searches for her vanilla pudding. After dispensing with all the sweets, the boy disappears into his hole and the tank goes the way it came. Under a green and brown thicket of trees at the edge of the yard, the children gather to eat.

In the folding chair, Mario stretches his arms above his head as if to touch the sky. A child's idea of endlessness. The humidity is unbearable, a heavy, wet weight. Or maybe it's the fire, still burning, throwing shadows on the wall of our building, shadow flames dancing in a tribal circle. The Makarov is in his hand again but nobody is paying attention anymore. He smiles at me, a sad lost smile. I'm silent. He points the gun at the side of his head again, slides his finger up and down the smooth curve. I close my eyes. Glass shatters brightly as somebody drops or throws a bottle against the concrete. Mario laughs. The crickets buzz like fire. Time is a river in the dark, Prof. Abdić once said, and we remember against its current. Before my eyes I see twenty pairs of legs run after one ball and kick at it blindly, hitting bone more often than rubber, while faraway adult voices hopelessly instruct us to spread out. I feel the warmth at my back. The sound reaches me before it's made. My eyes are closed. On the other end of the yard, opposite where I sit in my folding chair, the children silently and busily eat, chimerical in the tall grass. Tina gives up her search and walks over to where the others are. One by one she inspects their loot, finding nothing. She turns her bare feet toward her building as the crack of a rifle rings out. Then the sound of the bullet striking brick. Then silence. Huddled together in the high grass, the children wait for a sign to move. A few women stray out into the yard. Tina wipes the palms of her hands on her shorts. Overhead, the sparrows reassemble on the useless telephone wires.

When the time comes, it is up to me to chaperone Prof. Abdić back to the camp. I wait outside of his building for Mario to arrive with the car. When he does, we go upstairs together to the third floor, and Mario raps on the professor's door with the butt of his rifle. You are a selfish idiot, I tell him. He looks at me stupidly and hurt. The door opens and the professor greets us kindly, in dirty shirt and sweatpants, dropping his bagful of belongings on the floor and getting down on one knee to tie his worn sneakers, only the right, for the left has no laces.

Halfway down the last dusty flight of stairs, he suddenly stops. "I have to go to the bathroom," he says, his eyes fixed on the curved end of the banister.

"No, absolutely not," Mario says, pulling open the building door a touch, the light squeezing in like a cat. "Just hold it."

"Please, I must go."

"You should have gone before."

"But I must go now."

"Just let the man go to the bathroom," I say. Mario slams the door shut and leans against it. He lights a cigarette. "Let's go," I say to the professor.

"Thank you," he says in the doorway of his apartment, putting his bag down. His smile is childish, his green eyes moist and deep. I look away. "Give my regards to your father," he says, and goes into the bathroom. Hearing the click of the lock, I go down the hallway that has a door on either side and leads into the living room. Filled with light because there are no curtains, the living room is empty of furniture except for a couch and a makeshift table. The soft innards of the couch jut out through a rip in one of the red cushions, and the table is a shaded window glass laid on the flat seat of a backless chair.

On this table, along with a thick lilac-gray coating of dust, is a copy of Dostoevsky's *The Possessed*. I sit down on the couch and begin to read. I read for a while before I hear the hard, flat pounding of boots on the stairs outside the apartment, which I then can't unhear. I re-read the same sentence, word by word, but it reveals no meaning I can understand. The front door opens with a splinter and a thud. I throw the book on the table and run to the bathroom; in the hallway, I tell Mario to shut up and get away from the bathroom door. I put my ear to the wood. No sound. Prof. Abdić, are you ready? I say. No answer. I knock once, then knock again; I beat on the door with my palm; Emir, I yell. I turn the knob with force and the door gives easily. He lies on his stomach, heaped on the floor, a black puddle spreading from under his throat like velvet, like ink. The blade half of a straight razor glints coldly on the tiles. Mario drags his body out from between the toilet and tub and puts one hand over the other and pushes against his chest. His movements are slow and vague, as if performed underwater. He yells at me, tells me to do something. I just stand there. His hands sink slowly in and rise slowly out. On the wall, reaching the ceiling, a splatter of blood, dark as cooked jam.

I walk around my old neighborhood, hunching my shoulders against the wind. My boots hurt my toes as I walk. I turn toward Prof. Abdić's former building and run into the boys by the rosebush-flanked entrance, forming a circle around something on the ground; I yell and they scatter. Ringed by rocks that they must have gathered, the carrion of a small bird lies prone on the grass. One wing is spread out and the other half-covers its gray belly and dark throat. Its bronze head is turned to one side, the lead-blue beak slightly open. The bird is a sparrow. Ants are moving over its corpse, wrapping it in a quivering black blanket. I stare down at the diminishing sparrow. I feel the sun on my neck. The wind makes me shiver, but I keep staring. And if one of the boys happens now to come back, he will see me bent over and shivering in the sun, frozen like in a picture, and he will think I am shedding tears over a dead bird.

Translated from the Bosnian

7 June 1993

Dear Arabela,

They came for me like for any other, in the morning, knocking innocently. That freckled boy, the baker's son, frowning like a servant, and Goran, looking away and smiling the smile of the eternally blameless. I took what I could, what was left in the apartment, a suitcase of clothing and essentials, and walked in between them down the stairs. The courtyard was full of men with suitcases or rifles and the indistinguishable cries of women. They were rounding up the whole neighborhood, herding them onto buses, young and old. What a scene, Arabela, what a terrible and familiar scene, with that terrible and familiar disorder with which we do everything.

That was three days ago, I'm sorry I could not write to you sooner. But there is not much to write, not really. The bus drove us to Heliodrom, and after two nights in the sports hall I was put into a room on the second floor of the military college. They have boarded up the only window here, but sunlight peers in through the cracks in the wood. There are too many of us in the room, but that is to be expected, along with the smell, the heat, the restlessness and boredom. Mira's son is with me, as

I'm sure she has told you. He is doing fine, though I can feel my age against his impatience. He paces like a teacher. Today they brought in three more, including Mirsa, who stood in the center and asked what corner we use to piss in. We laughed, and so should you. There are toilets in the hall, there is food and water enough, and Goran is careless with his cigarettes. Life goes on. But to write about life here in more detail seems pointless, as absurd as describing the weather to you. Do not misunderstand my silence as a stoic withholding. And do not believe the gossip of Mira and the other women. They exaggerate; it is their right.

There are many of us here, but I keep to myself. So far I have been spared any labor at the front because of Jadranko. He says it is the least he can do and I'm beginning to believe him. My back only occasionally flares up, from sleeping on concrete.

Arabela, I miss you in the morning and I miss you at night. I miss the shudders of your body when you sleep. The murmur of your breath and its comfort. The animal sounds your stomach makes in the dark. I miss waking up to you still asleep, on your side, with both hands between your knees, in the silent radiance of our bedroom. I miss those mornings when you roused yourself with a sigh and came into the living room where I read, naked the whole flawless length of you, carrying in your hand your numb arm, fish-heavy and tingling with pain. I miss how you would let me straighten it out and rub it back to life, then kiss you from elbow to palm. Arabela, I miss you in the morning and I miss you at night, I miss and I miss.

Keep writing to me often. Take good care of the baby by taking good care of yourself. And after every breakdown, gather yourself and stand firm, Arabela.

I love you and always will,

Alen

Dear Arabela,

I remember. Of course, I remember. Behind my father's house, where the river narrowed with the willow trees on the banks, their boughs so close to the water that at the edges one could jump out and grab onto them, swing from them like the children did. And farther down the river, the old fishermen, catching trout and telling jokes as ancient as their bait. And you, your hips flickering in the green water, the white flash of your armpits as you swam.

I remember the summer Jadranko and his family went to Istria and left the house to us. Our weeklong imitation of marriage, you called it. Do you remember that? We lay in bed until noon everyday, in a chaos of sheets, listening to American music and eating from your brother's garden. Remember when we called "American music" all music that was not ours? Or French. You tipped the strawberries with whipped cream. I watched you eat.

Nothing has changed here, our lives go on. I worry only about Nermin, the powerful restlessness within him. The guards have begun to goad him. He talks about breaking out. Where will you go, I tell him. Mirsa says that the circus has come to town and we are its performers. The trapeze artists and fire breathers, tamable beasts. This cannot go on forever. We must come to our senses, while we can still look into each other's eyes.

Keep writing, Arabela. Do not struggle alone, write your pain down and I will feel it. But do not linger in pain. Remember to let your hands wander over your belly for me.

I love you and always will,

Alen

Dear Father,

Are your dreams still blameless? Is right still distinct from wrong? Like milk from blood, you said. Is the law still heavier than the cross, still the soil greater than the veil? You were always a man of logic and common sense, a Sisyphean passion, a faithless saint. You gave to your country until nothing was left.

In your heart you knew each man's vice, but you held them all equal before the eyes of the law. You said intuition is intuition but a law is a law. You were well regarded and treated each man fairly. You said charity is charity but a law is a law. Do not let them trample your conviction or poison your faith, you said. Do not let them turn you against your brother, for there will always be a wolf among the devoted hounds. And when misery comes to your door in the shape of a neighbor in uniform, do not let revenge turn your heart into a fist, because revenge is only revenge but a law is a law.

Father, you dreamed of a paradise on earth and believed it was home. I remember our walks together when I was a boy, the beauty you tried to impart to me, the pride. The rattle and crunch of our country roads, the soft tapping of the cobblestones in Old Town, how they amplified our footsteps, like we were a small procession of fathers and sons. Sounds of our land, you said. You lived for the smell of lilies, so overwhelming in the morning, for the sight of butterflies flitting over daisies and dandelions, a snail on a leaf. Sometimes, on our walks, your eyes would moisten, becoming a fainter green, almost transparent, and once I even saw a tear form on your cheek before the wind took it. You said no stone is just a stone in the country of your birth. You knew the names of trees.

Nothing binds a nation like victimhood and pride, but ours was bound by victimhood alone, shared wounds, a long history of the knife and the wire. For you, Yugoslavia was too logical of an idea to fail, inevitable and correct, an invention of nature. But you were wrong, father, our state was not a mountain, its law not a stream. You were wrong, not every pond within our borders was a watering place. Your laws have failed me. Your faith has deserted me. Your wrongs have wrecked my life. The nation you built has fallen into the nothing you built it from. Yugoslavia is dead. Communism is dead. Both died in their sleep, like you.

Sometimes I wonder about your ideals, father, if without them the wind would have blown you away. Communism, that hollow faith, that blackout among stars, what would you have been without it? Without the law you practiced all your life, the land you cultivated only in your dreams. Father, you logician and saint, you sensible and fatal man, with a soul full of ideals and landscapes, I hope you have now reached the paradise you thought your country to be, felt the love of a God whose indifference you were all your life indifferent to, and I hope you are at rest somewhere where rest brings happiness.

I love you, father, and can do nothing but love you,

Alen

23 June 1993

Dear Arabela,

I apologize for not responding to you sooner, but they have not let me see the doctor until now. I can judge the progress of the war by the mood of the guards. There is nothing new to report. I'm doing well. My back is only a little sore. I have a beard now. I have also gotten some new clothes from Jadranko, but they barely fit me. And the cigarettes he brought me are not my brand, though I can exchange them with Goran. There is nothing to write, Arabela, and I'm tired of writing nothing. I only live to read your letters. I cannot make my loneliness eloquent or my pain wise. I'm tired of trying. I'm tired of writing to an addressable but unreachable you, in only the language of loneliness and pain. I'm tired of memory and its clumsy echo. You tell me not to become desperate, to stay hopeful, yet all hope is desperate here. But you can tell from my handwriting that I'm calm. Should I tell you about the hunger that wakes me before the guards, the thirst which is much crueler, the humiliation of running in a circle while singing their songs. My feet are bruised, my skin hangs from my bones, and my asshole itches. My hands are dry and cannot make a fist. I lie in a small room full of shipwrecked men. I smell like an animal smells. But I will not cry out of guilt over you or pity for myself. I will not shed any tears for the living or the dead. Prison is a dry place. Three days ago I saw Nermin get beaten for spitting on the boot of a guard, get beaten until they could not beat him anymore, his teeth scattered on the ground, his mouth red and shapeless. I only chose one hell over another, mine over yours.

Dear Son,

I close my eyes and I see you as you might look someday when you read this letter, tall like your uncle, as handsome as your mother, with her beautiful eyes, her beautiful heart, her soul. I see you in the yard of the building that was to be your home, standing in front of it as if for a picture. I close my eyes and there you are, in your room, my former office, at the roll-top desk, my desk, reading this letter. The dark is intimate, but it is not home. I open my eyes and you are gone.

My son, I do not write to you out of guilt or shame. I do not write to explain my reasons for anything, to confess or repent. I write to give you a history of myself, so that you are not without knowledge. I write to keep you company, so you do not feel abandoned. I write to you to have a reason to write, my son, my son, my son.

You know where I was born, and when. You know that I was an only child. And you might have heard that my father, your grandfather, was nothing if not a good man. He had good looks and a good education. He had good taste, sonnets and sonatas. He was strict in his realism and his realism was practical and good. He was fussy and self-assured. Doubt and terror never assailed his mind. He was loyal to family, country, and the law. What else can I write? I did not know him as well as I should.

As a child, he took me on walks through the city and countryside. He spoke of the history of our land and pointed out its beauty. He never talked more than on these walks. From our house on the bank of the Neretva we would go uphill into the city. On Fejić, people would stop and talk to him, their gestures playful and exaggerated, their voices like the voices of actors. The cafés were full of men under tilted shade umbrellas calling out his name. We walked past mosques with their heavy gray domes and silent minarets, and father spoke of their beauty and their history and cursed their existence. Everyday we crossed one of the three main bridges, Lučki, Titov or the Old Bridge, depending on my father's whim, and went west toward Partizan Park, where he read while I played. Before going home, we would usually end up in some pastry shop on Avenija to have baklava with lemon juice.

On weekends, the family visited your grandmother's parents in Privorac. We walked through the copper and gold of pear groves, past tall black pine and down sunlit grass to the bottom of Hum Hill, climbing a gravel road only used by sheep and their herders. My father's voice mixed with the sounds of animals and it seemed to come from as deep within him as the humming of bees or chirp of the sparrows that trailed us for the breadcrumbs. On those walks I learned about the Romans, the Turks, the Germans. I learned the names of our hills, our birds and trees. I learned more on streets and bridges, in orchards and on riverbanks, than in school.

Do the street names remind you of home, my son, or are they unpronounceable?

Your grandmother was a storyteller and jokester. She told stories of ghost children that swing from clotheslines and of an oddly shaped boy who lives trapped in spoons. She told these stories in a voice eager and warm, larger than her body, gesturing like a magician. I remember my mother in long skirts and light-colored blouses, swaying in the kitchen, her bare feet moving to a song on the radio. She would roll her hips and throw a free arm in the air. And when a favorite of hers came on, she would grab me and dance me from living room to kitchen and back, our naked feet turning in the amber and blond light coming through the beech leaves.

What I will miss the most is never seeing you run crying into your mother's lulling arms, never hearing her voice grow husky with endearments for you.

The rain is wrinkling the windowpane, my mother would say. She called butterflies the drunks of the air, said their frantic wings were as silent as ghosts. She compared the yolk frying in the pan to the sun simmering in the sky. The blue of the sky blazes, she would say. She made up stories about the lovers who carved initials in the pale-mottled bark of the beeches outside of our house, myths of eternity and longing. Both my parents wanted to describe their world to me, to show me the lurking wonders in familiar things.

Now I want to share some of that beauty with you. So you, my son, can see the house in which I grew up, the wooden porch in the backyard, my mother hanging out the wash on the clothesline, my father sitting with a book under a willow by the water. To see your mother carry a basket of vegetables and crouch down by a slow river, see her run through a pear grove, disappearing behind branches and waiting to be found.

I do not know you, my son, but I know that I love you, and is that not the height of love?

Your Father

25 June 1993

Dear Arabela,

Do not give me terrible news I already know. I saw it with my own eyes and the memory of it torments me. There could not have been much life left in him when they dragged him away. I understand you want to be with her now, to bring with you a miracle for her, but Mira does not need you and your wanting to be of use would only make you stand more in the way. Nermin is gone from this world but he will never be lost to her.

Do not add to my troubles by writing about a return. You are safe where you are and I will join you soon. Just write to me for now. Tell me more about your life and ask me less about mine. I only live to read your letters. Tell me if you have gone swimming. Is the saltwater stinging your lips? Are the mosquitoes pitiless? I know how you would rub your ankles against the rough edge of our bed at night. I remember the spider bites on your thigh, small and round, pale as scars. Keep writing about the life that is inside you, make me feel the shudders of his body. I imagine how big you will be when we meet, like there is a globe under your shirt, the whole world, Arabela.

Write, keep writing, write longer. Be true to us by never straying from yourself. I kiss your roughest knuckle, your belly and our child.

I love you and always will,

Alen

Dear Son,

I met your mother in Makarska, though neither of us was staying there. A friend and I had rented a room north of Makarska, in a smaller and cheaper resort town; your mother and her friends farther south along the coast. I cannot describe to you, my son, the first time I saw her for when I looked at her for what I thought was the first time, in a café, dipping a sugar cube into her coffee, I realized that I had seen her before, that I had passed her on the promenade, had noticed her on the beach. In the café she was sitting off to the side, by herself, yet somehow the center of everyone's attention. This I noticed repeatedly, her proud and unapproachable solitude. She was lonely but unconcerned. She was quiet, which was intimidating because it was rare. She was tall and held her body straight. There was something of the aristocratic Russian about her, the long dark hair, her pale face, my imagination. From one of her friends I learned that she was involved with a tourist, an American. I imagined a rich older American with a summerhouse in the Adriatic, but it was only a young backpacker, rugged of build, blond of hair, from Montana. She called him Montana, never telling me his real name when she spoke of him. I never asked. She said she liked foreign men because she could change the meaning of her name with each new man, because foreign phrases of affection were easier not to mean.

Each morning I took the first bus down to Makarska and walked on an empty beach until I felt ready to call her. Together, we would walk up and down the promenade, then get coffee in the Old Town square before meeting up with our friends at the beach. She had a car and was more flexible than me, but her vacation was almost over while mine was indefinite. She could make me wait, I realized, and leave me with nothing. It was only on our very last day together that she told me that in a month she would begin studying at the University of Mostar. We had gone up some hill to see an old church there, and from the church took a path through the forest to the statue of St. Peter, which overlooked the town, the red roofs of houses, the glint of traffic. It was morning, the sun low above the Adriatic, violet and orange spread out over the horizon. She touched the key St. Peter held in his hand and I took a picture with her camera. On the walk back she told me about her plans, as though she did not know or had forgotten that I went to school there too. I could not make her aware of it again, for fear that she would not care. I tried not to show my hurt or anger and so became indifferent. Your mother had eaten an orange on the way to see the statue, and now I saw the orange peel she had left behind, mixing with pine needles and cigarette butts on the ground, stirring in the breeze. Birds sang overhead, sharp, rapid notes, and small yellow butterflies darted above lavender shrubs. But she talked about her studies and her talk ruined everything.

The sundress she wore that morning was white and there was a yellow sweater tied round her waist. I remembered because I thought it would be the last time I would ever see her. Mostar was a big enough city not to run into each other, and the History building was miles away from Language. We stood on the cracked stairs on the top of the hill, ready to descend, when I told her that I would stay up here, lean against one of those graying church walls and read, patting my pocket as proof of the book that was not there. She gave me a look, angry, annoyed, but obliquely affectionate, coy. I resisted it, said that I would rather stay and read. She rolled her eyes, large and brown; who are you fooling, they said. She offered me her hand, but I ignored it like a shadow. Her features slackened. She told me then, in a voice tender and unforeseeable, that I would never understand her feelings for me. That is when I knew, almost too late. My son, I was a fool with your mother and lucky to get her, lucky the way only the foolish are lucky.

I will not describe to you our relationship in all its meanderings, but there are some things I want you to know. Your mother will tell you the rest, if you let her. We dated for a year and it was summer again. I worked the fields with your mother's father like a character out of a Russian novel, my neck burning. We picked Marasca cherries in the morning, the sun slowly rising behind the high boughs of maple trees, blurring their leaves. Her family accepted me as one of their own. And when her brother's family went on a trip to Istria, he left the house to us as a responsibility and gift. We borrowed from his garden and stole from his cellar, selecting the wine by the thickness of dust on the bottle. The house was near the Buna River and we bathed there under a moon perched on a hill. On the terrace, which was overhung with grapevines, we danced drunk on another's wine and our own love.

We were married in September of 1990, the ninth, and moved into an apartment on Rude Hrozničeka that the Yugoslav Army had given to my grandfather for his service in the second World War. After I graduated, I got a job in the food division of Velmus, a wholesale distributor on the outskirts of Mostar, where I eventually became manager of the warehouse. Your mother and I bought oil paintings from local artists and hung them on our walls. Copper plates of the Old Bridge and watercolors of pomegranates we put in the small room adjoining the bedroom, your nursery. We filled colorful bowls with colorful fruits, oranges everywhere, a habit of your mother's that had turned into a pleasure. She had begun eating them when she was young only because their smell covered up the cigarette smoke in her room, on her skin, her fingertips. We drank coffee three times a day, together in the morning and evening. Your mother started teaching at my old high school as part of her praxis and I began working ambitious hours to justify my promotion. Then, one dawn in April, the war started, a slow dawn whose colors were not gentle. The year was 1992. Hopeful people, we blamed the violence on circumstance and history, ancient grievances and long memories, a bad economy, the fall of communism.

We went from basement to basement, ending with a relative of your mother in Bijeli Brijeg, not far from the stadium. It was a large house with a large basement, a view of mountains from the balcony. I drove to work each morning until the Serbs overran the warehouse. Your mother never denied me the normalcy of our former life. Survival is not complicated, my thoughts or your mother's thoughts as we crouched under stairwells or hid ourselves in pantry closets with the sugar and potatoes. And when the Serbs left, there was nothing simpler than to return home and pick up the pieces. Our apartment had been plundered, each cabinet door in the kitchen flung open as if out of breath, but we had not lost anything that could not be replaced.

If it had not been for you, your mother would not have left when the war began again. You saved her life. Remember that. I cannot explain to you what happened next, because I do not understand it myself. They came for me one morning and I went.

Your Father

Dear Arabela,

   You will never be lost to me. You are not near when I awake, but I embrace you in my dreams. You are far from my touch, but my arms stretch out patiently toward you. We are apart now, but I have never felt closer to the place where we will meet. I will wait and listen for you there. I will move in the direction of your voice, always. As long as you have memory and language, speak my name. Do not let it become a ghost between your lips. My heart beats within yours, Arabela.

   I love you and always will,

Alen

29 June 1993

Dear Son,

I knew that another war would come, that the Catholics and Muslims were turning against each other. Everybody knew, though your mother and I tried to keep it a secret from each other and even from our own selves. And when the war did come, what else could I have done but wait until it was over? There was nothing to fight for because to fight for a city is to destroy it. There was nowhere to flee because there was no hope for me of life beyond my land, beyond the small patch of Mostar that was mine. Anywhere but here, the longing for what I had left would have exhausted me, the instinct to return disturbed my dreams. My heart is anchored here, and here it must be buried.

That is all, and yet it is not enough. I feel that I have failed to make myself understood. It was your fate, you will say. You must forgive me for leaving you with nothing but this letter, small glimpses of my past, cracks of light. You must forgive me for leaving you.

I think of words my father said to me, words I can pass on to you. Never turn your back on your country, your grandfather said. But you will only appreciate the unintended irony of that. Be good and you will be happy, he said. But he also said that I should be good even if it makes me unhappy. He said, Do not resent what you know is necessary. My son, do not hate those whom you should pity.

Forgive me for having the last word and leaving you the silence,

Your Father

September 24 2011

Dear Father,

A response to your letters is not needed, but it feels natural to write one, more natural to have it in the form of another letter. Maybe response is the wrong word. We write to the dead what we did not remember or dare to say when they were alive. We write to the dead because there is always something more we want to say. My need to write to you is not much different.

Sometimes I'm angry with you, and sometimes I pity you, but most often words are useless to describe what I feel for you. Mom has kept you alive in my mind; there are pictures of you around the house, there's one I particularly like. You two are standing on grass under the raw branches of a bare tree, a Bosnian maple, and there's a river in the background, green and inert. The Neretva River, mom said, and complained that nature always appears startled in photographs. You're wearing a brown jacket and dark pants, your expression is stern and remote, your mouth doleful. The slight flutter of mom's skirt is evidence of a ghostly breeze.

The letter you wrote to your father and the letter you wrote to mother but didn't send, the one where you describe prison as a dry place, were found in a shoebox along with letters from mom to you and a black-and-white picture of her. There was also a leather case for glasses in that shoebox, a wristwatch whose battery had given out at a quarter to nine, your passport, driver's license, and other documents proving your identity and existence. They were saved by Uncle Jadranko and given to mom when she returned to Mostar, nine months pregnant, to bury you. She came back to Split only a week after your death because she could not stay in the place you had died for longer than that. My life is ruined there, she keeps saying. Whenever she talks of you she starts crying with an intensity that embarrasses me and makes me proud.

She added the letters she had received from you into the shoebox and stored it in her closet. The shoebox lay there for years, not exactly hidden and not exactly put there to be found. She'd show me the letters when the time came, and it came a few days before our trip to Mostar. I was twelve. I remember that first trip back as a series of cemeteries, destroyed buildings and unknown family members fawning over me with a delicate cheerfulness. Nothing is rebuilt, mom said, pointing at what used to be a shopping mall. There was trash everywhere, and graffiti on the walls of ruins. There were buildings with only their façades standing, hollowed out with trees growing inside and branches shooting out of empty windows. It looked like an abandoned city, left to nature, but at night people came out into the cobbled streets of Old Town and cafés filled with music and laughter. But it's a city divided in two, on one side the church, on the other the mosque. Even the dead are divided, though you, father, are buried in the city cemetery, which is common ground and, ironically, just outside Mostar. We stayed on the eastern side, the Muslim side, with Mira and Izudin, even though this angered mom's family. She didn't care. She rented a car and showed me the sights she wanted me to see: our old apartment, the houses of both of my grandparents, and the Old Bridge, so crowded in the summer, with divers walking the ledge and teasing to jump. On the last day of our trip, on our last visit to the cemetery, our last walk down the cement path to your headstone, we lit the candle we had bought you and placed fresh flowers on your grave. Then, for the first time, mom kneeled in the dirt, put her palms together and improvised a prayer. As we walked back to the car, she spoke of the immense human silence of a place like this that made it possible to hear the wind rustling in the trees, the birds chirping on the branches. Like the silence of a silent crowd, she said.

After we returned from Mostar, I reread your letters. I began listening more closely to our songs, began learning the history of our country, from books, from my mother's mouth. But still I felt no closer to home. After a year in Split, we had gotten a visa to the United States and came to Phoenix, where there weren't many Bosnians, then to Tempe, where there were even fewer. The immigration agency had said Phoenix is your new home and mom didn't complain, because she didn't care. We moved to Tempe because of her job. I grew up an American and mom didn't care about that either. And Mostar we visited only because she wanted to see your grave again. She will visit often, but she will never come back for good. Whenever I read about war in books or see documentaries about it on television, there's always the feeling that those who had lost their homes or a loved one, even those who were wounded or raped, were somehow lucky. Maybe it's an instinctual reaction by the onlooker, but it strikes me as the wrong one. He was wounded but at least he survived, they'd say, like survival will cure all pain. She was raped but lucky to be alive, they'd say, as though only the dead are unlucky.

I can't explain to you how I could miss a place I never knew and that never was my home, but I began missing Mostar with an unexpected urgency and regret, the way I have always missed you. I told mom I would go back after graduation, and she agreed. I took your letters with me and went for a month this year. I stayed with Mira and Izudin, in their downstairs apartment in Old Town, where mom and I had stayed before. Every morning I went for a walk to the store (Mira refused money so I filled their refrigerator in compensation) and each walk would take me to stores farther and farther away. It is hard to describe the adrenaline I felt on those walks, how swift and tireless my legs felt, how the beating of my heart propelled me forward. The sky was a deep orange in the east, a pastel blue in the west, and the cobbles gleamed like they were wet. They amplified my footsteps. I heard the clutter of tables being set up outside the many cafés, the scrape of chairs, and the *whoomp* of blossoming shade umbrellas. I heard the voices of young shopkeepers bargaining in English and German where Fejić becomes just an alley with souvenir stalls on either side. I heard the beating of wings as pigeons fought for breadcrumbs thrown by an old man on a bench. Walking on Fejić, I smelled spinach pita and burek from the bakeries and the milky batter street vendors swirled into crepes on their hot plates.

After lunch, Izudin would speak to me about local and international events, beating the newspaper with his forefingers, the toothpick in his mouth forcing a smirk on his large, good-natured face. He told me stories about being a soldier on the wrong side of the Neretva, hunting farm animals for food and stealing supplies from UNPROFOR, told me how some of the people responsible for his son's death are still out on the street. The Hague is but a poor man's Nuremberg, he said. He spoke like a comedian, but there was pain in his eyes. We are a funny, careless, and bitter people, he said. Everyday he asked me to translate a peculiar and impossible Bosnian phrase into

English and everyday he laughed at my literal and nonsensical translation. At night, on the weekends, I hung out with Izudin's nephew, Edo, who showed me the nightlife of Mostar, which spanned ethnic divides but was otherwise unspectacular, not any different than in America. Though before each night out at the club we'd go to a small and isolated clearing in a beechwood forest, where young men and women would come to drink bargain wines from gas stations, sitting on logs and rocks while music from their car stereos and the lilies of the forest overwhelmed the night. It was something mom said she did when she was a teenager, something you probably did, too, and something now I have also done.

One day, I met Uncle Jadranko in a large café on the western side of town, not far from the rondo. The streets on the west side have all different names now and mom's directions were nearly useless. The architecture is modern and lifeless, but the cafés and shops are crowded. Jadranko looked much older and smaller than he did when I last saw him, his face wrinkled and nut-brown. He spoke passionately about his house on the Buna River and his dream of retiring there soon, smoking cigarette after cigarette as he spoke and flexing his brows with every exhalation. He still works for the city council. I asked him to tell me about the Heliodrom camp. This is what I learned: he worked nonstop to obtain your release and had you just given him more time, you would have been freed; he got you out of working at the front, digging trenches and building fortifications for the army that imprisoned you; it was through him that you were granted access to the doctor, who was another prisoner, and to the small but comfortable room within Heliodrom where patients were kept. There you lay on an army cot, writing letters and waiting for your back pain to subside, and there you hung yourself from a drainage pipe on the last day of June with a length of rope you used as a belt. I'd known all of this before. I also know that human shield is a beautiful combination of words, that freedom is the horrible feeling before you make a decision, and that there can't be any redemption in keeping a man alive if he wants to die and no redemption in letting him die.

Jadranko and I argued about the check until he leaned back in his chair, giving up. When the waitress came, I paid her while he shook his head, playing with the cellophane wrapper of his Camel pack the way his sister does with her Marlboros. When I returned to Mira's it was that bad time of the day in Mostar when temperatures hit triple-digits and it's unbearable to be outside. I usually spent those hours listening to music or reading in the cool of the downstairs apartment, but that day I took out your first letter to mom and started translating it, because that day it became impossible not to try.

Each day during those dead hours between noon and dusk, I worked on the translations, trying to make the letters as beautiful and affecting in a new language as they are to me in the original. Each day I tried to dig through to you. I failed because failure is the translator's fate, because every note on translation is a somber one. I failed because there was too much earth and language between us. The more of myself I transferred into the letters, the more of you I lost. What's left is only a ruin in translation.

On my first visit to Mostar, with mom, the Srebrenica tapes had just been released, and footage of the massacre was shown frequently on television. It showed Bosnian Serbs drinking and joking while the prisoners they had rounded up squatted in the background, waiting to be shot. It showed Serbs firing into the mountaintop forest through which some of the men tried to flee to safety. It showed the terrible ambiguity of safe areas. It showed a man shouting his son's name to the mountain, forced to tell his son to give himself up, that nothing would happen if he did. The son's name was also Nermin, and hearing that name groaned by the father, like from the bottom of a ghostly well, made Mira hysterical for days.

The footage also showed the actual killings, the men being dragged from the back of trucks and made to kneel on the grass, their hands tied and heads down. It showed the events of Srebrenica with the most detail and clarity possible. It brought them closest to reality for the viewer. But what I wanted to know as I watched the footage was more than the camera could show, more than any anthropologists can tell. What I wanted to know was the men's thoughts as their knees hit the ground, what each one was thinking the moment before death. That the camera cannot capture. The bones do not reveal.

I love you, father, and can do nothing but love you,

Alen

The Last Castle

The first time she appeared was three days ago. She walked across the field, her white dress waving sideways in the wind. Visitors of any kind were strictly prohibited ever since the sport hall's transformation into a makeshift prison. It was an unwritten rule and therefore strongly enforced. Yet there she was, steadily approaching. He stood up bearing his rifle and walked out to meet her. He asked what she wanted in the same careless tone he used with all the women, whether he knew them or not. He knew her; they had grown up in the same village. She told him she wished to see her husband, and he told her that it was impossible. She didn't seem to understand. None of them did. He told her to go home and turned his back to her. He returned to his seat by the entrance gate. She repeated her request, but he didn't pay her any attention. She stood in her spot, staring at him. He let her. After an hour, she left.

***

I stood with my back to the mirror, looking over my shoulder, staring at my reflection. Like a character about to be described, my mother thought, standing in the doorway behind me. The room, her former girlhood room, had one wall lined with books, most of them novels, or *romans*, as she still calls them, *Jane Eyre* and *Anna Karenina*, Austen and Dickens, de Balzac. My mother had read a lot when she was younger; then she'd have appreciated seeing herself in a story. I'm the age now she was when she read all those novels, too young, maybe, too eager, too inexperienced to tell her story right. I don't possess the omniscience of old age; such gift has been granted to my mother, at least in regards to me. Even now, far from each other, miles and mountains apart, I feel that she knows what I'm thinking, knows that I'm writing about her.

Once upon a time my father went on a business trip and didn't come back for three months. This is how I meant to start, disguise her story in the rags of my fairy tales. My mother and father read them to me before they turned out the lights, fairy tales with handsome princes and virtuous princesses, perilous journeys and heroic quests, propitious returns, happy endings.

Or I might have continued the way I'd started my first telling of this story, her story, from his perspective, the other man in my mother's life, a fable: He looked out at the field, watching two boys kick a ball back and forth while a girl stood in goal, leaping after every shot and each time disentangling the ball from the back of the net. He wondered if she'd come today...

Instead I will start with my five-year-old self, looking into the mirror, seeing my mother reflected there. I have chestnut hair, curly at the back, green eyes, and freckles on the bridge of my nose. I'm wearing a white dress with blue flowers on it. My mother is adjusting the strap of her own white but flowerless dress and scratching a cheekbone with the back of her thumb.

"Come honey," she says, taking my hand and leading me out of the house, down the wooden stairs that do not creak.

That's how her story begins.

In the yard, my grandmother was pruning her plants while Albi, the son of her next-door neighbor, stood near at hand, holding a translucent green watering can whose neck was curved like that of a swan. I can't play right now, I told him in a matter of fact tone. Because I'm going somewhere. He shrugged. I didn't tell him where I was going, because I wanted to keep it a secret from him, but also because I didn't know. My grandmother had round and dusky cheeks; she smiled at me but the smile faded when she looked up at my mother. She wore yellow gloves that seemed a size too big, probably my grandfather's. They spoke for a while, my mother and grandmother, while I joined Albi by the watering pump, which looked like a rooster to me. The spigot was rusty, chipped, and gleaming; Albi was pulling at it ineffectively. He was beginning to become interested in where we were going and I was pleased by that. I told him he'd never know, that he'd never get it out of me. I was glad to be able to keep a secret; it thrilled me to do so. As an adult I still keep my secrets close, even the most insignificant, especially those.

I went with my mother when she called me, waving with my free hand at Albi and my grandmother. We walked up a gravel road that had a blazing strip of grass running down the center, old, modest villas on the left, quiet woods on the right, which gave way to a cemetery on a small hill. The cemetery seemed to have as many trees as headstones, the trees creating a leafy tent over the ground, letting in only thin, fuzzy strobes of sunlight. Grasshoppers whipped themselves haphazardly out of the grass onto the white cement path, and we sidestepped them the best we could. A harsh wind blew; it was the season of strong winds.

I didn't reach out to catch the sticky leaves that flew toward us as I usually did. My mother felt the squeeze of my hand tightening as I bravely read the stones. She read them, too, only the dates, smiling at the long, robust lives, frowning at the heartbreakingly short ones. How sad and absurd, she thought, the story of one's life rendered by a date, by a few innocent numbers engraved on a stone.

"There's nothing to be afraid of," she said to me. "We're just visiting grandpa."

"Albi said that the dead sometimes come out of their graves."

"Nonsense! Albi is lying, honey. The dead do not come back."

We arrived at my grandfather's grave, which was in the shade, as he'd have preferred. The headstone was arched and made out of granite. On the stone's ledge, neatly arranged, lay flowers—my grandmother's bouquet of roses and my mother's own solitary, crown-shaped pink tulip inserted into the neck of a green wine bottle—an unlit votive candle in a silver candlestick, a tiny brown teddy bear gifted by me, and a locket with a black-and-white photo of him inside. My mother kneeled down, pressed one palm against the other, inclined her head, murmured an abridged prayer, and thought how useless all this was. She crossed herself, certain that she was doing it the wrong way. Three fingers bunched together or was it just two, tap first the forehead, then the right shoulder, then the left, and then under the ribs, or was it the other way around?

How useless!

She made it a custom to come to her father's grave every day, improvise a prayer and depart. The maintenance of the grave she left to my grandmother, who would've been devastated if ever deprived of that duty. Mostly she came alone, sometimes with me, but rarely with my grandmother who had the habit of talking to her husband as though he was still alive, which infuriated my mother, who must have seen it more as a sign of dementia than devotion. I admit it scared me sometimes when my grandmother spoke to my grandfather. How could he hear her buried under all that earth? Then I felt guilty for not talking to him myself, but whenever I tried, my mother told me to stop. Then I wondered if Albi was right and I was afraid even more. My mother also disliked the fresh tears that my grandmother shed at each visit. My mother still felt the pain she'd felt right after my grandfather's passing—a pain that numbed her body like a piece of driftwood and filled her mind with a silence deep as the sea—but she could no longer cry, which meant that my grandmother cried because she felt an even stronger pain, or that her tears were automatic, unreasonable, ultimately meaningless. Either possibility frustrated my mother.

"Take it out," she said to me when I placed a blade of grass into my mouth, wanting to roll it between my lips. "I'm warning you, take it out." I pushed it out with my red tongue.

My grandfather had died from lung cancer, even though he'd never smoked in his life, a life that could be summed up in few concise sentences, "he never smoked" being one of them. He worked at the army cafeteria his entire life, and he always brought home some kind of treat. Candy bars or liquorice for her, leftovers for the pigs that had absurdly attached themselves to my mother's memory of him. She remembered three of them when she was eight, their broad ears, their nighttime squeals, and the flies, the multitude of flies, orbiting them like satellites. All three pigs, big and burly, were crammed into a small, filthy stall made of stone. My grandfather once caught my mother staring at the pigs and told her not to get too fond of them, bound as they were for the butcher's table. Don't give them names, he'd said. But my mother hadn't the slightest intention of naming the pigs and felt nothing for them, nothing but cold fascination. Everything they did, which wasn't that much, they did in a slow, sluggish manner with the same pig-stupid expression on their pig-ugly faces. But if comfort were to be measured by degrees of indifference, indifference to one's existence and to the dignity of the self, then my mother knew, even as a child, those pigs were the most comfortable animals in the world.

She remembered finding it disgusting how comfortable they were in their dirty skin. Then she thought of the man, not my father, but the man who stood between her and my father, the man she wanted to push through. How disgusting he was in his skin, in his fatigue pants and tawny undershirt. His physicality, the frankness of it, repulsed my mother. His face, the hairs on his arms and chest, his bloodless gut, his stare. As ignorant as a pig, but pigs didn't know better. Ignorant, she thought, but full of purpose. Had he always been like that? Even before the war? With that sulky mouth and those resentful eyes? Just like that, only younger?

My mother turned her head to the side, saw me on my haunches, reaching out an arm to touch an amber and black butterfly perched on the tulip in the wine bottle. It flew away and my eyes watched it bounce and skim the air. My mother smiled, thinking how large the world must have seemed to me, how large and generous with its wonders. She got to her feet, brushed the grass and dirt off her knees and the hem of her dress, tucked a strand of hair behind her ear.

"Now we are going to see Daddy," my mother said, taking me by the hand again.

***

The next day she was back and the whole scene was rewound and replayed. Ignoring her, it turned out, didn't make her go away, but only prolonged her stay. He was surprised, charmed. The barbed wire shone in the rain that fell. She asked if she could see her husband and he said that she could not. She stood in her spot. And even as the sky darkened and the light rain began pouring hard, she stood there, she stayed, buttoning up to her neck the thigh-length brown jacket she wore over her white dress. Her icy stare persisted, and she asked again from time to time if she could see her husband. Soaking wet, she left after more than an hour.

***

Had my mother woken with her desperate plan or had she gone to bed with it hoping to change her mind by morning? Had she remembered the night's inspiration at breakfast the way you remember a dream that you then cannot shake? How well did she know the man to take such a chance? She knew him by sight, she says, a familiar stranger in a small village, a face in the hall. Did he know her better than she knew him? Was there a dark admiration in his distant gaze? Did she know if he had children of his own? Where is he now, I want to ask my mother, though how would she know? And why would I even ask. Your father is here, she'd say, and so are you.

I urged my mother to stop at a playground we were passing and she allowed it. Three swings and a square sandbox, that was it. And we were the only ones there. I walked over to the swings, my fingers gripping the rope, and began to swing, kicking up wood chips in every direction as I pushed off the ground, gaining speed and height. Opposite the swings, my mother sat on a wooden bench painted white and watched me, her legs crossed. When she was my age, my mother would build up a lot of speed and get as high as she could, and then, with a mighty forward thrust, jump off. Nine times out of ten, she would land on her feet. She still enjoyed swinging, but now her feet kept brushing the ground and she just couldn't hold her legs straight in the air anymore without them starting to throb and sting. My mother missed how her feet used to dangle when sitting down as a child. She missed the pure and empty space beneath her toes.

And what, my mother wondered, would I miss about my own childhood? Hadn't she painstakingly recreated at least the illusion of the life we'd had before the war? But wasn't she now going to blow that illusion into bits and pieces? It was I who'd heard the knock on the door, opened it to find three soldiers asking for my father. It was I who then ran into the bedroom where my mother and father were taking an afternoon nap, leaped on the bed and burrowed in between them and woke them. My mother told me to stay in the bedroom and closed the door. Knowing what their arrival signified, she pleaded with them not to take my father away. She told them she was a Christian, but it made no difference. My father kissed me, my mother following him down the stairs of our building after locking me in the apartment. When she came back, she braced the back of a chair against the knob. The next day we went to my grandparents' house.

My mother watched me swing, unable to forget his leaving, unable to cleanse her memory of the image of him getting on a bus with the others, a suitcase in his hand, a bag over his shoulder. Nor could she ever forget the blunt simplicity with which she explained to me my sudden fatherlessness. Daddy has gone on a business trip, she'd said without hesitation. It was what they used to say to children during communist times when the secret police took someone's father away. When my mother says we get over pain with age, what she really means is practice.

"We have to go, honey," she said, standing up. "Don't you want to see Daddy?"

We reached a street lined with small linden trees, a street whose old name had been changed. We slowed our pace, strolling on the sidewalk. Ants moved swiftly in the cracks of the pavement. We passed a florist, looked at a batch of tulips. Some of the tulips were entirely yellow, others entirely red, and there were a few, my mother's favorites, which were as pink as a fingernail. We moved on, past a bakery, the pleasant, peppery smell of bread escaping through the open door, then a shop that displayed in its window, in whose plate glass we were reflected, an expensive-looking set of dishware. My mother eyed a gold-rimmed soup tureen while I tried to pull her away. We heard the distant shelling only when we paused to listen to it. At a small boutique we both stopped to stare at two cream-white mannequins lit like on a stage: a woman wearing a black pantsuit and a girl in a red dress. Mother and daughter, my mother thought.

"Like looking into a mirror," she said.

"But she's not wearing a dress," I said, my freckled nose pressed against the glass, my breath befogging it. We continued our stroll, watching the few cars that drove up and down the sun-drenched street. The pigeons cooed, stout and long-necked. They clucked.

"Though Daddy has come back from his trip," my mother said suddenly, looking straight ahead and swallowing hard, "he still can't stay with us because he is busy at the sports hall." She paused and glanced at me. I was scratching the bump of a mosquito bite on my arm. She waited until I was finished. "He's so busy that he might not even see us today, so please don't become upset if he doesn't. And there is always the possibility of another trip, you understand?"

I merely nodded at the words my mother had released like a breath held too long.

We turned into a cobbled side street, where restaurants occupied either side. The restaurants were empty in the early morning, but music could already be heard from the inside. The wind blew in the narrow street, shushing the music. We were taking the long way to the sports hall because my mother made it a point to only pass through the parts of town that were relatively untouched by war. Even those parts of town must have looked different to her now, changed in some imperceptible way only she could tell, changed by survival as by death.

I pointed at the kiosk we were walking toward. "Look, a cat," I said, but my mother shrugged her shoulders unable to see it. "Right there," I pointed again at a yellow ice cream box next to the kiosk. Strutting out from behind it, there it was, a muscular brown cat with a milky white chest. My mother allowed me to play with it, wanting me to be momentarily distracted.

"Two Marlboros and a newspaper," she said through the little window to the man inside. Seeing that I was busy hissing at the unimpressed cat, she quickly added: "And also that candy bar over there, please." The cat was licking its paw and I was as bored with it as it was with me. I took my mother's hand gladly and we walked on down another cobbled street toward the park. I asked what was in the paper bag and she told me, leaving out the candy bar. My mother didn't even know what kind of candy bar she'd bought, but it was small and flat, which would make it easy to conceal. The plan was to pass it to my father without me knowing so that he could then give it to me as a gift from him. That, my mother was certain, would make all the difference.

***

The next day she was there again, white glistening under blue skies. This was the third day in a row, her coming as certain and unfailing as the sun's. There she was, first curling her dark-colored lips into a frown and then giving him the precise, icy stare he had come to expect. She asked to see her husband. Annoyed suddenly, he told her that they had hanged him three days ago. She looked like she didn't believe him. He went back to his seat, leaning the rifle against the fence and laughing to himself. She remained rooted to her spot, her stare unfocused, standing there with the dignity of a ruined sculpture. Then she left.

***

We walked across an open field, our white dresses whipped by the wind, strong but warm. Firs stood on one edge, with smaller trees farther down where the field sloped toward the fenced entrance of the sports hall. In these smaller trees cicadas made a sound between a hum and a drone. The man my mother knew from the village, in fatigue pants and tawny undershirt, came out to meet us. What an ugly brute, my mother thought, carrying his rifle as he approached with the sly, compulsive movement of an animal. There were two other guards there with him, a young man with a deep slouch playing cards alone and an older man with gray hair and beard, asleep. Behind them rose the square hulk of the sports hall they were whimsically guarding.

Their eyes, my mother's and his, were fixed on each other but yet there seemed a great gulf between where their ultimate gaze lay. He glanced at me only briefly, smiling as he did. He held his rifle like one does the handle of a suitcase. The sky overhead was clear, blue as chalk.

"I wish to see my husband," my mother said, and to this day I remember the plaintive tenderness of that plea, like a meant prayer.

"I told you that it's impossible. I told you this just yesterday."

The intensity of my mother's gaze didn't fold. She asked again, and as she asked the second time, she gave me a small nudge forward so that I was almost in between them, this strange man and my mother. He glanced at me again, no longer smiling. The young man with the slouch leaned against the chain-link fence, watching us while he shuffled his cards. I bowed my head. My mother wondered if the barbed wire atop the fence, bright as copper in the sunlight, had always been there, and if it was, how come she'd never noticed it before. She stared back into the man's eyes and didn't find there the resentment she'd expected. In the silence between them all I heard was the stiff shuffling of cards. It stopped when the man called to the younger one to get my father. It had been a long time since I'd heard my father's full name spoken out loud.

My mother took me by the wrist and we left the man standing there, watching us leave. We sat down on the grass near a patch of daisies with which my mother let me play. It gave my mother pleasure to turn her back, even briefly, on this man, to not feel, at least for a moment, like a leper. She tried not to make eye contact with him anymore, though she knew with her whole body that he was looking at her, holding his rifle and staring like at something hard to see.

A few minutes passed and my mother thought it strange how she could wait calmly for hours when there was absolutely no prospect of seeing my father, but how as soon as there was the slightest promise of his appearance, every second became unbearable. She stood back up again, while I sat hunched forward, my elbow in my palm, winding flames of hair around my finger. To my mother I looked lost in a world of my own, a little white statue with enchanted fingers sitting in the gold and yellow glimmer of sun and grass. She took a few nervous steps, keeping an eye on me. The way she kept her eyes on me was the way the man kept his on her. His head moved with her movements. She crossed her arms over her chest, to protect herself from his gaze, holding in her hand the brown paper bag. She felt his stare and sometimes she stared back, imagining the glowing red mark her hand would have left on his cheek had she not resisted the desperate urge to slap him yesterday. A butterfly landed on one of the daisies, the sunlight flashing through the translucent amber of its black-lined wings. My mother stopped her pacing, pondered the purity of my concentration as I slowly reached out my hand to catch it.

My mother began pacing again, thinking of all the darkness and light in this world, all the immense darkness and beautiful light in the universe, and how none of it was holy.

On one part of the field not far from us, where a goal stood, two boys and a girl had gathered to play. My mother paused to watch them. The taller of the two boys gave the ball a prod to get it rolling and, running up to it, powerfully kicked air. She heard the man laugh behind her, and thought bitterly how these kids' games were probably his only entertainment when the prisoners' wives weren't here. She kept watching, though, enchanted by their play. The taller boy gave the ball another prod and ran up to it again, this time hitting it hard. The ball blazed wide. He ran after it while the girl got off the ground and wiped herself clean for the umpteenth time.

My mother watched the kids so intently that she didn't notice me getting up and going over to the man who had called me. He put down his rifle and bent toward me, one hand on his knee, the other drawing something out of his pocket. Whatever he took out, he hid behind his back. I heard my mother cry out, a choking gasp of a sound that ripped through his whispers.

"Come here, Ana," she said harshly, pulling me by the sleeve of my dress.

"Wait!" the man shouted. "I just wanted to give her something. Look, Ana."

He glided his hand over a crudely made fist several times, gesturing emphatically like a real magician while muttering *abracadabra* in an embellished accent. I let out a long sigh when he revealed a candy bar in the palm of his hand. It looked vaguely familiar to my mother; she didn't have to open the paper bag to realize it was the same candy bar she'd bought.

"She doesn't want it," my mother said.

"But Mom—"

"Be quiet, Ana. She doesn't want it."

"She obviously does, but you won't let her have it," the man said, with such vicious force that I ducked behind my mother and clung on to her dress. "Why don't you let her decide?"

This he said more softly, with a note of regret in his voice that was more revolting to my mother than his anger. But she felt compassion as well; hope had made her compassionate.

"Okay, Ana," she said, without emotion, "take it."

The man crouched down, offering me the candy bar; I stepped up to him, swaying forward, scrutinizing the candy. I looked up at my mother, then stared into his palm again, my own hands lifted but inert, ready to grab, but not grabbing. I dropped them and shook my head.

"You don't want it?" he asked.

"Uh-uh" I said, still shaking my head.

My mother picked me up, wrinkling her nose at the scent of my curls, and we walked in the direction of the field. I buried my head in the hollow of her neck, holding on to her shoulders. She turned back toward the sports hall but could no longer see it clearly. The man dissolved in front of her eyes. She tried to watch the gate, but it too dissolved. The trees, the field, the sky, everything seemed to be dissolving, melting away in the warmth of her incomprehensible tears.

***

This is where the writer in me wants to end it. But then I remind myself that this isn't fiction, not all of it, not even most of it. At this point my mother's story isn't yet complete.

When my father came out that first time, I ran to embrace him before I even had time to register his appearance. Only during later visits did I realize how thin he was, reminding me of a mirror without a frame, how hard and dry the knobs of his knuckles were, how brown the back of his neck had become, how long his hair was, dark hair that he kept sweeping back from his dark forehead and darker brows. By his appearance alone I should've known he was a prisoner, and maybe at some moments I did, only to become distracted again and forget. I should've known by the fact that at every visit he gave me candy even though it was clear that he had very little to eat, mostly the food my mother had begun bringing him. She brought food for him and he brought food for me and I didn't see any contradiction in this giving. I saw nothing in it that wasn't right.

Fact presumes truth, maybe, but the lowest kind.

I didn't visit him every day, like my mother did, just enough to never feel the full weight of his absence. Eventually he was released and finally returned home from his trip. We left for America soon after that. My mother tells me that she didn't have the courage to believe the man when he told her that my father was dead, just as she didn't have the courage to believe that bringing me to the prison was wrong. Maybe she simply didn't have the courage to lose faith, whether in God or man. Why would I ever want to begrudge her this lack of courage? What forgiveness should I offer my mother for her faith? If I was in her place, I'd have done it, too.

My mother weaved a world in which I was caught and cushioned, a world of bare threads cleanly interwoven where I couldn't tell illusion from truth. All the knowledge I have acquired can't reveal their differences now, nor can dark memory, with its dimples of light, like water at the bottom of a well, or like the pupils of my mother's eyes through which I have tried to see.

Admir and Benjamin

Everybody always said that Admir was crazy, but to me he was just impulsive, rash, a child with grown-up tastes. If somebody asked me if he was intelligent, I'd pause, then say he wasn't stupid. But if somebody asked if he was passionate, I'd respond without the slightest hesitation—yes, Admir was always hiding behind his passion.

He was broad-shouldered but fragile looking, rolling his shoulders as he walked, head held high, short, dark hair flattened to his scalp like he had just come out of the rain. From afar, his face seemed to consist solely of a forehead, though a closer look revealed a small nose, a brown mole under the left nostril, a sensitive mouth and strong jaw. And if you looked closer still, you would notice within the pale blue of his eyes, around the pupils, a burst of green. But only few ever dared to come that close to Admir.

Almost a year has passed since Admir's murder, and some Bosnians avoid talk of his death while others have genuinely forgotten it. Igor, in jail and awaiting trial, still maintains that he had not meant to kill Admir when he stabbed him outside the pool hall, and I believe him, not that it matters. A few days after the murder, in the garage of one of Igor's friends, Admir's blue Mitsubishi Eclipse was found, and then sold.

Almost a year has gone by but Admir is still constantly on my mind. He's in my dreams and nightmares, and I remember our past together with a poignancy both pleasurable and sad. A poignancy that arises when moments shared by two people can be invoked in memory by only one.

***

Admir and I met at a bus stop, on the first day of 7th grade. We were introduced by my cousin, Amela, at whose apartment my parents and I stayed for a month after our arrival from Sarajevo to St. Louis. She was eager to hand me over to somebody else and Admir turned out to be a great guide, navigating me through the halls of Buckley Middle School, translating my teachers' slowly spoken instructions and my fellow students' slang-filled talk. Outside of school, he continued educating me on the codes and customs of American adolescence. What clothes to wear and how to wear them: long, loose shirts and baggy jeans worn low to reveal your boxers. What kind of rap music to listen to. How much gel to put into your hair.

I remember the time he showed me how to play baseball, first explaining the complicated rules with the aid of a video game, then taking me out on the tennis court in our apartment complex and teaching me how to properly grip the bat and swing it. "Hold on to it this time, Benjo," he'd say, then duck after throwing the pitch. I recall how he smiled and shook his head when on the third day of our lessons I arrived with a newly bought, right-handed glove and was unable to throw a single ball on target with my left arm, scattering yellow tennis balls, our substitute for baseballs, all over the red court.

My parents and I moved out of our relatives' crammed quarters into the building across the street from them, into an apartment one floor below Admir. The fact that we were the only Bosnian boys in our apartment complex made our friendship almost inevitable. With who else could he play catch, throw a football, kick a soccer ball; with who else could he exchange confessions of shoplifting and masturbation, confessions that only showed our lack of anything to confess; to who else but me could Admir describe, with a fortuneteller's vagueness, his deepest dreams and desires? That we never talked about the war is only significant in retrospect, but our silence meant that he never heard about the bullet that lodged in the refrigerator door as I was rummaging for something sweet inside. And it was only by accident—overhearing my parents' conversation in their bedroom—that I learned about the Serb who held a knife to Admir's throat, only a bribe restraining him from murdering my best friend.

Knowing what I knew scarcely altered my perception of Admir then. It did soften his faults and made it much easier to forgive him when, after having had a fit of temper, he promptly came by to apologize. He was particularly upset about defeats in gym class. He had to win every game, and when he didn't, he would blame my poor play for the loss, though he kept picking me to be on his team. But what did it matter, the anger he sometimes showed toward me, it could not change our need for each other. We accompanied the girls to the nearby theater on South Lindbergh—which played movies already available on video—and played in the pool with them all summer long—but their lives were lived apart from ours. They gave one another meaningful glances that we could not decode, laughed at jokes we did not find funny, and we could only guess how many times they had gone to the movies without inviting us. Admir liked

Amela, and I liked Esma, though I can't tell now what separated them from the other two, all four blond-legged and flat-bellied, with dimples appearing when they twisted their lips into smiles. Even their personalities were similar, an infantile cheerfulness that could and would change with nightmarish abruptness into a pubescent girl's gloom. We adored them in a subdued, languid way, and in that same way they ignored us.

Our isolation and longing were never more apparent than on the December night of Amela's thirteenth birthday, celebrated in the form of a slumber party—girls only! To kill the curiosity we felt, Admir and I had a sleepover of our own at his house, one that must have rivaled theirs in excitement and fun, though it merely consisted of us kneeling by the window and peeping through Admir's binoculars—he hunted with his father—at what was happening across the street, at that fantastic and mysterious twilight gathering of girls. It had snowed all day, but in the evening the snow ceased, granting us a clear view into my cousin's room—before the curtains were drawn. But we held our positions, sustained by the nervous pleasure of expectancy, passing back and forth the binoculars, drinking coke and eating chips and hoping for a stir in the curtains, which would give life to the larger hope that they were secretly peeking at us too. By the yellow rectangle of light that bordered the greenish curtains, we knew that they were awake, which meant that they were talking, about us maybe, though we doubted it. How cruel it was to talk about them all the time and think that they talked about us never.

An hour passed and nothing happened. The snow gleamed blue in the moonlight, and the sky was the color of plums. Snow-crusted branches gave the grim shade trees a beautiful frosted glitter. The curtains did not stir. The light in the room below the one we were watching winked on and off twice in quick succession. Icicles hung blue-gray from the roof, and snow, windblown off the building, swirled out into nothing. Another hour passed; the green curtains did not stir.

It was not out of boredom but from excitement brimming over that we decided, wordlessly, through a series of glances and smiles, to get dressed—thick pants over our plaid pajamas, hooded jackets and knit hats—and go over there. The wind singed our faces and gushed into our mouths as we slowly crossed the street, Admir walking behind me so to step on the indentations I created in the snow with a crunch and make it appear as though only one person was taking the journey. Once inside the building, we stomped our feet on the potato-colored carpet longer than was necessary to get rid of the snow, then went up the stairs, laughing out of anxiety and joy, and shoving each other against the gray metal banister and tawny-spotted wall. By the door we fell silent. We knew, by the light, that they were awake. We also knew they were alone, at least for a while, because Amela's parents were over at my house to give the girls the illusion of privacy, which we now desired to destroy. A knock would probably do it, but that seemed mischievously simple, like an easy question asked by the teacher that nobody in class dared to answer, fearing it was a trick. So we just stood there, putting our ears to the door, hearing nothing but our own heavy breathing.

Suddenly, Admir pounded twice against the door with his gloved hand. He stared at his arm with open-mouthed astonishment, as though it had moved on its own, then he looked at the door, then at me. Thin, angry voices rang out;

rapid footsteps approached the door. He took a step back, panic etched on his face, darkening it, turned and ran off, the stairs booming woodenly, the downstairs door opening with a screech and closing with a slam. I stood alone in front of the nightgown-clad girls, their faces identical in their bleak expressions, all four barefoot. It was at their feet, small, soft-looking, and white, that I stared at as I tried to explain, the door shutting before I could finish.

Starting home I was angered not just by Admir's eventual cowardice but also by his initial bravery. I never saw it coming, the knock, having thought that we had wordlessly agreed not do anything but linger for a few more exhilarating moments and then quietly leave. His knocking and running were equally terrible, and I was angry because both actions excluded me.

Entering my building, our building, I found him sitting on the stairs, his head bowed. He looked up only after a while, his cheeks burning. I gave him what I hoped was my most hostile stare, and in return he smiled. Looking at that smile, the blazing red cheeks, his upturned, sheepish eyes, I could not restrain myself any longer and burst into laughter. Soon we were laughing together and could not stop. Then we went back upstairs, and in the warmth of his room, with our cokes and our chips, I started to tell him all about the four dreary faces and eight ivory feet.

***

In middle school I could have counted on my fingers the number of Bosnians, while in high school I did not get to know them all even after an entire year. Milton High School was a series of connected brick buildings, low and rectangular, with the cheerless, formidable demeanor of a prison. Two long, blue metal benches flanked the main entrance, and it was on those benches that the Bosnians would congregate every morning. I never contributed much to the conversations that would sprout and tangle like weeds. The predominately banal chatter—gossip discussed in an inarticulate hybrid of English and Bosnian—perfectly captured the dull personalities of most of the people there. Certain mornings I was absolutely ready to believe that they, the blank-faced boys and gaudy-painted girls, did not really exist but were only part of my lousy imagination. Or, more accurately, that they were part of my first fumbling attempts at character construction, vivid on the outside but on the inside empty, the kind of characters one finds in the drawer-bound works of young writers.

The only reason I sat on those benches and remained sitting there until the bell rang, as opposed to stealing away to class or disappearing in the library, which had acquired a sudden grace after I had read my first book, was Admir. I was naturally inclined to be wherever he was. We spent less time together during high school, and when we were together it was usually in a group, before somebody's house, for example, assembled around the raised hood of somebody's car, bent over the shiny engine, examining it, as the owner sat behind the wheel and blissfully pressed the accelerator. Or it was on the basketball court where I would slide and slip and bump into everybody, the ball slyly slipping out of my hands when it mattered most. Each Friday night he dragged me to some terrible bar in South City or to the pool hall on Gravois where music drowned out any attempt at conversation. When we did spend some time alone, I found that our friendship had not changed at all since the early days, and though he had changed, just as I had, I still felt the same way toward him—I was still charmed, hurt, and occasionally bored by Admir.

I was charmed by his passion—for music and sports, cars and women—a passion that might embarrass a stranger, but which was utterly charming to those that knew him; by the childish fondness he had for food, even taking pleasure in watching other people eat; and, especially, by the pain and pity he showed at the sight of some unhappy animal. (Sophomore year he adopted a large, burly, brown-furred dog that constantly knocked into the corner of things, tipping over chairs and small tables, but who also raised his paw with such an intelligent and endearing inclination of his head.) Yet Admir was intolerant of human shortcomings, and though he was sympathetic to the pain of others, sometimes he did not detect its existence, or his own contribution to it.

He often spoke to me about what he proudly called his girl-related problems. One day, as he went on and on about his most recent girl, an American, I realized that his problems were all entirely similar in theme. What he was essentially complaining about was his girlfriend's inability to get over his cheating on her.

"I don't understand why she's making such a big deal." He was sprawled on the red sofa in the corner of the room, Rambo, the dog, by his feet. "Why can't she realize that just because I hooked up with that girl doesn't mean that I don't love her anymore."

"You know lust isn't love." I sat in an armchair, across from him, by the window.

"I know that. I really do love her. But why can't we just fuck whoever we want, even if we're in a relationship?" The dog glossed his black nose with his long mobile tongue. "She shouldn't be so uptight about it. Why does she even care?"

"She cares because she's a human being," I almost yelled, and he just shrugged without taking the slightest offense.

What bored me about Admir was a trait common in the self-absorbed Bosnian male—a morbid lack of curiosity. The pleasures he had discovered at twelve became the pleasures he enjoyed at eighteen and beyond, not adding anything new, not even trying a more complex version of the same pleasure. I persuaded him to read some books I had specially chosen for him, but it was useless, though there was a funny moment when, after he was confidently given *Slaughterhouse Five*, he earnestly asked me if it wouldn't be better to read one through four first. He wasn't enthusiastic about the music I tried to get him to listen to either, though it was still a pleasure whenever we listened to our old favorites.

Admir loved rap, wrote down lyrics, had dreams of becoming a rapper. And it was partly in tribute to 2Pac, his favorite, that Admir had tattooed "Soldier" across his chest on the night of his seventeenth birthday. "Soldier" because, as he explained later, this is what we Bosnians are and will always be. I smirked at that idea and also at Admir wearing a star and crescent on a chain—this was probably another effort at copying rappers, only with a star and crescent in the place of an electric chair or tank. That Admir was sincerely religious never entered my mind. I simply did not believe that he believed. But then came visits to the mosque and hard fasting on Ramadan, and I decided to casually ask him if he really believed in God.

We were in his room again, Rambo and I on the sofa, Admir on the armchair, sitting in profile toward me and looking out of the window. He was unaccustomed to fasting, and one could tell how miserable he felt at being deprived of breakfast and lunch. *All Eyez on Me* played softly, and in the velvet hush between the end of one song and the beginning of another, I asked.

"Of course I do," he said, not breaking his bleak admiration of whatever he was looking at outside.

"So you believe in heaven and hell, too?" I asked. He nodded, and kept nodding as I explained, through the horrible paradox of human freedom, the impossibility of heaven or hell. I stopped talking after he had stopped nodding. He didn't appear to be listening, staring, it seemed, at the glass and not at what was beyond it.

"Admir."

He turned toward me, blinked. "I see your point," he said, "but I still believe that there's a heaven, and a hell."

I felt as though I was the one fasting. Could he really believe in something so strange, something in which I couldn't? "And do you think you will go to heaven?" I asked, sarcastically.

"I do," he said.

Then I asked, not sarcastically, but in a tone unintentionally gentle, if I would.

"Of course you will," he said, smiling indulgently, the way one smiles at the questions of a child.

***

In senior year of high school we both began to do the things for which we would become to be known: I began to write stories and Admir began to get into fights. That year I enrolled in Honors English, taught by Mr. Humphrey, who always wore horn-rimmed glasses and Hawaiian shirts, and part of the requirement for passing the class were two original compositions of either fiction or poetry. So it was mostly out of necessity that I wrote my earliest story, an immigrated teenager's first-person account of a war-tarnished Bosnian childhood, in particular his near death by an accidental bullet.

As for Admir, he had always been aggressive, and there were here and there a few fistless scuffles that resembled wrestling and were never endowed with blood. They arose out of trivial arguments, mere misunderstandings between friends, and Admir would never, no matter how angry he got, strike a friend over a trifle. But Eric Bynes was not a friend of his. An obnoxious moron, Eric had on the first day of senior year shouted "Speak English!" as he passed through the no man's land between the Bosnian benches. Unsure about whether he was being serious or just unfunny, we reacted only by shouting back at him to shut up. And so it went the next time he did it, and the time after that. But the fourth time, which would also be his last, was different.

As soon as he got out of his car and started walking toward the entrance, there was a lull of expectancy on the benches, and our collective stare must have seemed to Eric like a dare to shout out his stale two-word slogan again. He stopped just short of the entrance, in whose dark glass doors we were all duplicated, turned toward one bench—the one I was sitting on—and like a doll whose chord had been pulled repeated the only words he knew. Then he laughed through lusterless teeth, reached for the door handle but could not open the door—Admir, who had leapt off the opposite bench, had pressed his hand against the glass.

They stood silently face-to-face, Admir blocking the door and neither backing down. A half-circle formed around them, while some, like me, got up on the benches to watch, the crowd's excitement increasing as the silence endured. Eric finally said something, short, indistinct, and with a smooth, sudden forward motion Admir head-butted him. I heard a crack and tear, then saw blood dripping out between Eric's fingers as he tried to cover, first with one hand, then also with the other, his smashed crimson nose. He was bent over with his face in his hands and Admir knocked him down to the ground with a punch to the side of the head.

Moments later Admir was escorted by security to the principal's office, where he spent the morning. And when I entered *German III*, a noontime class we had together, he was nowhere to be found. The rumor at lunch was that he was suspended, and this rumor, spread by some not without a certain sense of pride, turned out to be true. I saw him in the evening; he was calm and said without going into much detail that he had been suspended for two weeks, that what Eric had said to him just before being head-butted was "queer"—which rhymed with an American's incorrect pronunciation of Admir's name—and that even if Eric hadn't said "queer," he would have still fought Eric because he did not like it when somebody told him to speak English.

I told Admir that he had overreacted.

"It's just that when somebody tells you to speak English," he said, "they are not only criticizing you for being Bosnian, they are also criticizing you for not being American enough, you know?"

I did know. I knew more than I let on.

In the aftermath of the fight, meetings were set up between school officials and Bosnian students, all of them male, to discuss urgent matters, including how to reduce the violence already characterized as rampant by our principal. These discussions took place in a small room around a large oak table, and two days into it my name was mentioned and I was requested to come in. What I found interesting were the four or five different motives dreamed up in that room for why Admir fought with Eric—out of jealousy, out of pride, even for profit (that Admir was paid to do it)—each motive tinted by the presenter's unique interpretation of Admir's personality. It was extraordinary to me that there should be evoked so many versions of one seemingly uncomplicated person, and even more extraordinary how for a majestic instant these different versions merged into what was, perhaps, a passing imitation of the real Admir.

On the day of the last meeting, a week after the Admir-Eric bout, another brawl occurred, this one in the cafeteria. It was between Cameron, a big black kid, and Igor, a skinny Bosnian. I did not like Igor, a.k.a. Rogue, amateur rapper and petty thief, who made terrible mixtapes and burgled the houses of other Bosnians. We all wondered how he really got the money for the Escalade he drove. He was auburn-haired, with a claw of hair falling over his forehead, tall, lanky, with deep-set brown eyes, prominent ears, and a crooked, broken-looking nose.

Descriptions, even of murderers, are so very innocent.

On our ritual night out the following Friday it took a real team effort to tell Admir about all the incidents that had occurred in his absence—the fight itself, the nervous intercom message of amity immediately after the fight, the school-wide assembly in the gym a day later, and all the ridiculous overreactions in between. We were at the pool hall and Admir seemed more interested in finding a free table than the information.

There would be another fight, in the spring, on school grounds again, this one between Admir and Cameron, ending with a broken jaw for Cameron and leading to an expulsion for both. (Admir would eventually graduate from one of those schools with metal detectors at the entrance, where fights were as common as French fries in the cafeteria). I did not see the fight and Admir only said it was about a girl. The rumors were more complicated and dark, and many thought that Igor was somehow involved. That it was some kind of revenge. It was after this fight that everybody began to say, shouting, whispering, with proud smiles, with respect, even with fear, that Admir was crazy.

Around the same time I wrote my second story, following the Marić family, dark father, blond mother, and three sandy daughters, as they attempt to cross from Bosnia into Croatia, their journey including an encounter with a Serb soldier who almost slits the throat of the youngest daughter. The other students in my class liked it, Mr. Humphrey liked it, but neither their comments nor the story's real merits could match the intense private pleasure I felt at having gracefully buried my friend's secret into one of my stories.

***

After high school, Admir and I began to occupy different worlds. We had different friends because his stayed the same; our interests were different because mine changed. I worked at the library and Admir worked in a car repair shop; I was a junior in college and he wasn't. Sometimes I even wondered if the little contact we still did have was not a naïve, unconscious effort by us both to keep alive the spirit of a shared past through occasional interactions in the present, as though ending our friendship would amount to treason against our younger selves.

We became close again in a way following the theft of his Eclipse right outside of our apartment building. I drove him to work and back for a week, while he fumed and plotted in the passenger seat. The police had come, taken all the information, and left promising nothing. Nobody had seen anything, of course, but Admir had a list of suspects, most of whom were his friends. I was the only one he could trust now, he told me. He'd be making some house calls, he also said, unambiguously.

One day, as we were driving home, Admir was uncharacteristically quiet, kneading his chin and staring intently out of his window at the gas stations and fast-food restaurants that lined Lindbergh Boulevard. He was probably sliding his tongue over his teeth, as he always did when in deep thought. I asked if anything was wrong and he shrugged. A vein, red at the base, swelled diagonally on his forehead.

"Can you drive me to Igor's house?" he said suddenly.

"Now?" I asked.

"Yeah, right now."

"For what?"

He sat up in his seat and spread out his arms, waiting for an answer. "Are you going to drive me or not?"

"Admir, what are you going to do?"

"I'll know when I get there."

"Figure it out now."

"Are you going to drive me or not?"

We arrived at Igor's house in ten minutes—he lived on Forder and Lemay Ferry, not far from where we lived. It was an ordinary ranch-style house, with a garage door painted bright green, and trimmed bushes under the windows resembling rows of teeth. There were no cars in the driveway as we entered it, no gleaming black Escalade, and I thought with relief that nothing would come out of this. The silver knocker was a thin ring in the clutching jaw of a lion. The screen door opened with an elastic twang and Admir held it open with his foot.

"Wait," I said, as he grasped the ring. "What if his parents are home?"

"His parents are in Bosnia, have been for a week. Okay? Will you relax?" He knocked on the door. There was no sound, inside or out, except for the incessant ticking of the cicadas. Kitchen fumes—a mixture of sausage and bacon—seeped out of the open window of the neighboring house. Admir knocked again. Nothing. "Go check the back real quick," he said. I checked the back: six patio chairs, a table with a shade umbrella, and a pool filled with floating leaves. No clothes on the clothesline.

"Nobody's there," I said, coming back. "He isn't home, we should go."

Admir knocked a third time. A bee flew by my head, its shadow on the door, the window-ledge, on a leaf, gone. A dog began to bark somewhere nearby.

"We should go."

Admir gave me a sidelong glance, smiled, and knocked again. I heard light footsteps, and Admir heard them too, cocking his head and bringing it closer to the door. They ceased, then resumed, but swerved to the left, away from the door, then ceased again. The curtain rippled. Admir, fingering his chain, hastily tucked it under his shirt when the knob began to turn. The door opened and a slim girl poked out her blond head.

"Who are you? What do you want?" she said, blinking in the sunlight. She spoke slowly, her voice throaty, hoarse. Judging by the lack of an accent, she was American.

"Is Igor home?" Admir asked.

She stepped out a little farther and glanced suspiciously at us both, scratching her elbow. Her face was unfamiliar, pretty, with pale cheeks and drooping blue eyelids. She was dressed in pajama bottoms and a white T-shirt. "Nah," she said.

"Well, can we come inside and wait for him?" Admir asked, gently pushing the door open as he spoke and stepping inside. "We're friends of his."

"I don't know when home he is going to come," she said, and then started laughing like she had the hiccups. "I don't know when home he is going to be," she said, throwing herself on the couch, laughing harder. Then, as suddenly as she had started, she stopped laughing. Admir and I exchanged looks; he formed a circle with his index finger and thumb and pantomimed smoking a joint. The smell in the house corresponded with his guess. I sat down in a recliner opposite the couch on which the girl lay spread-eagled, pouting at the ceiling, then at me, pink nail polish on her fingers and toes. In between us stood a wooden table, ash stained, with a sugar bowl in the center. The left-hand side of the room was taken up by a big screen TV, above it an oil painting showing the Old Bridge in Mostar, where Igor was born. Admir stared at the painting, rocking on his heels. He was born there, too.

The girl turned onto her stomach, propping her chin on her palm, and started talking about a movie she had recently seen. So we talked, she and I, about our favorite movies, past and present, while Admir walked through the house, rolling his broad, broad shoulders (broader than ever), and from time to time lifted a corner of the curtain to glance outside, making a triangular glare appear on the large screen.

Eventually, cross-legged on the carpet, he joined our conversation, turning his head toward the window whenever a car drove by the house until, after a whole hour of waiting, the right car finally came, announced by rap song and interrupting the girl's charming and incoherent description of some plot.

Admir stood up. The fear that hibernated through our conversation now awoke inside me with a roar. He was by the door.

"You don't know if he did it," I said, speaking in Bosnian, "so, don't be stupid."

"It'll be easy enough to find out," he responded in English.

"What did you say?" the girl asked.

Igor entered, eyes wandering, smile forced. "What are you guys doing here?" he said, offering Admir his hand.

"My car got stolen," Admir said, not shaking it. "You know anything about it?"

"No, how should I?" Igor brushed back the claw of hair from his temple. Our eyes met and I looked away.

"Someone saw you in the neighborhood around the time it was stolen."

"Who saw me?"

"My mother," Admir said, bluffing well. "On her walk. What were you doing?"

"Just seeing a friend." Igor tried to navigate past Admir but was blocked. "Will you let me go? You can't just come in here and accuse me of shit." He shuffled his feet, his upturned palms pleading at hip level.

"Where's my fucking car?"

"I don't know."

"Where is it?"

"I don't know." Igor took one step back and grabbed the doorknob. "I had nothing to do with your car."

Admir struck him in the face and the girl screamed. He struck him again and the back of Igor's head banged against the door. Then Admir hit him in the stomach.

"Stop it, Admir," I shouted.

Igor was doubled over, hugging his stomach, coughing. Admir relaxed his arms and just stood there looking at him. Suddenly, Igor lurched forward and fell to his knees, then face down on the carpet, still holding on to his stomach. Admir stepped over him and exited the house.

I told him that we were not leaving yet, so he waited outside while I helped the girl take care of Igor. His mouth was swollen and bloody, and his right eye, also swollen, was a blue-rimmed slit. I told him that he did not look all that bad. We sat him on the recliner, and with McDonald's napkins found in the kitchen we cleaned his face while he groaned. The girl then put an ice pack to his face, bending over him and, every now and then, removing with her free hand a bit of hair that kept getting into her eyes.

Outside, Admir was leaning against my car. "Did you exonerate yourself," he asked, rolling his eyes at the word. I said nothing. What could I say? Wasn't that exactly what I was doing?

Later that same day, a phone call disrupted my writing; home alone and writing, I let the machine pick it up. The vague message, given in a moist hysterical girl's voice, was clear enough. I did not try to call Amela back but drove straight to St. Anthony's. I remember the yellow-painted waiting room, and certain conversations I had but not with whom I had them (there were a lot of people there). I remember pouring paper cup after paper cup of bland, lukewarm coffee, and then I remember a short, chubby man, an uncle, announcing to the room that Admir was dead.

***

The funeral was held in November on a sunny afternoon in a small and treeless cemetery in St. Louis. I was sitting in the second of five rows, at the edge, not far from the coffin, dressed in the required black and austere in my expression of sorrow, though my hands trembled, slightly but visibly. Admir, his skin a dusty blue, his hair slicked down as in life, his features softened as if by sleep, seemed to me the only flesh-and-blood being among all these spectral figures.

The same short, chubby uncle that had announced Admir's death delivered the swift eulogy. He was also round-headed and bald, this uncle, with prominent cheekbones and small eyes, resembling a turtle. The eulogy started off with some details of Admir's childhood in pre-war Mostar—including an anecdote of how Admir once ran away with a pig and hid with it in the nearby forest to rescue it from the butcher's knife—but then degenerated into general statements that could have been made about anybody.

Admir was described as good-hearted, hard-working, independent, truthful, and loyal, though he was, at times, the very opposite of those things. And sometimes he was also impulsive, impatient, and primitive, but one was forbidden from blemishing the dead with faulty human traits. Therefore the Admir being eulogized was almost alien to me, a half Admir, an Admir painted exclusively in bright colors and so unlike anything found in nature. All light and no shadow. It was then and there, among the mourners, listening to the eulogy, that I decided that I would write about Admir. And now, as I'm writing the epilogue to my own version of his eulogy, I find myself overcome with doubt about everything I have written, certain that I have failed to describe Admir as he really was.

I see him on the basketball court, shirtless and sweaty, passing the ball flawlessly through his legs, pivoting with a squeak of his sneakers and flashing past an opponent, his strong, outstretched arm laying the ball in the basket with a sharp pump of the palm. I see him in the yard behind our building, being chased by Rambo and laughing. I see him behind the wheel of his car, strangling the gear stick and screaming as we race down an empty highway at four in the morning. I see him in my room, fidgeting to a song, his hands swaying like a conductor's. I see him standing by a dark door—eyes bulging, mouth forming an O—that winter night he ran away, that winter night when I, not for the last time, was left behind trying to explain.

Hand in Glove

The job is simple. It's the setting that's complicated. I go from business to business in South City, St. Louis, and ask owners to sign partnership agreements with the Census, which they do without reading them. I ask them to distribute pamphlets to their customers. To advertise the Census by keeping engraved pens and buttons on their bars and counters. I ask them to put up posters of smiling families on the walls of their restaurants and cafés, Bosnian stores that sell Bosnian brands reminding the Bosnians here of what they have lost without truly replacing it.

When my parents returned to Bosnia a month after I graduated from college, I was supposed to fly out with them and help with the renovation of our old apartment. A half-expected call from the Census Bureau changed our plans. I drove them to the airport on Friday—my father satisfied, my mother hopeful, neither of them happy—and on Monday started work. What I had in mind was going door to door in a South County neighborhood helping people fill out their Census, asking them questions by which strangers define one another, listening to the answers that told nothing. Instead they made me the Bosnian Representative and sent me to South City.

***

My family and I came to the U.S. in the summer of '95, after three years in Germany. We came to St. Louis, where my uncle had lived since the start of the war. He was our sponsor, a key word in the refugee vocabulary. He picked us up at the airport and I remember the drive to his apartment with remarkable clarity. My uncle's Dodge smelling of hot leather, the lunar-cratered roads, a bumpy ride, sunlight, low buildings, lots of sky. I was eight. I remember my mother and I sitting in the backseat, looking out of the same window, and her crying at what she saw.

After half a year at my uncle's, my parents bought a house on Evergreen Lane in South County. We lived there for almost fifteen years, until they moved back to Bosnia and I got an apartment of my own. Most of our neighbors on Evergreen Lane were old. There were two widowers, both dead now, who played chess on their porches every day but Sunday. They'd greet me with gray lingering smiles when I came out to check the mail or mow the lawn, and I'd think that the only thing the old know with any conviction and insight is that it's better to be young.

I know things now I did not know then. How both of the widowers sometimes resembled Dr. Gachet in Van Gogh's famous portrait. How painful the decision to buy a house and how drawn out and stressful the process was for my parents, how hard they tried to hide the anger and regret that came with every refused loan, every realization that they would not return to Bosnia anytime soon. How, in the faces and hearts of young and old, patience is always melancholy.

***

Throughout high school I didn't tell anybody I was gay. I walked the halls separated from my true desires, sitting in the front of classrooms, meticulous and aloof. There wasn't anybody I felt comfortable enough to tell, certainly not any of my Bosnian friends. Only Nina, but I had no faith she'd keep it to herself. I knew she'd be the first one I'd tell once I was ready, and I imagined her looking at me afterwards with the same expression of recognition and disbelief with which she stared at the wall in class.

I had met Nina in elementary school. We were in Ms. Armstrong's class, the only Bosnians. She was a little tomboyish then, but our relationship was uncomplicated. We were children. In the snow, we slid down swift hills, secure and warm, invulnerable, in our thick clothing. We went to the pool in her apartment complex and played baseball in a nearby park, Nina and I in the sunny outfield, excited, nervous, a little dreamy—a dream from which the hollow thud of the aluminum bat woke us. Yellow grass looks red in the sunlight, she said once, with that random precision of hers.

By high school even I had noticed the changes she'd undergone and could no longer ignore the vulgar appreciation of the boys around me. Her sexuality seemed most apparent when she was dancing, in the flicker of her hips. She wore knee-high leather boots with everything, spoke of *candy* photography and *handsome* cabs, and at parties passed out with a cigarette in her mouth, knowing she had me to take off her boots and put her to bed. A mediocre student, she depended on me in class, when she wasn't faking an illness to get to the nurse's office. I enjoyed the warmth of her when she leaned over in Mythology class to ask in a loud whisper: What are the names of those sea monsters? Syphilis and Chlamydia? I thought we wouldn't have traded in what we had for anything, even for the possibility of something better, even if we could.

***

I spent the summer before senior year in my room, dreaming of college. Nina came over from time to time to keep me updated on what was happening in my absence. There wasn't much I was missing. She was excited about the upcoming school year, about being a senior, about a big party one of the Bosnian girls was going to throw in August, to initiate us into that glorious year. But I was indifferent to its promise, didn't care. There was no convincing Nina, however, who leaned back in the armchair with the look she wore when dancing or dreaming and imagined a year of unmatched excitement. I smiled without condescension as I listened from the bed, thinking that we all need to fool ourselves a little.

The night of the party she sat in my room begging me to go. She'd had her long boots propped up on the table but was now pitched forward in the chair, worried that my no's were serious. She was sitting under the fan, its wooden blades cutting through the smoke from her cigarette. On the bed, I lay with my arms behind my neck, looking at the pockmarks on the ceiling. *The Queen is Dead* played low on my computer, over the murmur of the air-conditioning, the insect whir of the fan.

"It won't be the same without you."

I laughed. "It'll be exactly the same."

She put out her cigarette in the ashtray in her lap and tipped out another by tapping the bottom of the Marlboro box. "You sure your mom or dad won't suddenly barge in?" she mumbled, cigarette in mouth, lighting it.

"No, they'll be gone for a while." Smoking was not allowed in my house, or coming into it with your shoes on, but Nina was special. The ashtray was a secret between us, hidden in a locked drawer with some lyrics I had written to nonexistent songs and the scrap of a story I never had the heart to throw away.

"I have to, you know, keeps my fingers busy."

I smiled.

"Come on, please."

"I really can't, Nina. I just don't want to."

She got up from the seat and lay down on the bed, putting her legs over mine. The ashtray wobbled on the mattress with every shift of our bodies. She wore blue jeans and a dark shirt that had "HORSES" across the front of it in glitter. The shirt bared her midriff and reminded me of all those times she tried to wear something similar to school and was caught by the authorities and given a jacket with our school logo to wear over it, which she did proudly. It reminded me of the tight skirts that slid up her legs when she crossed them a little more dramatically than she should, semi-drunk at a party.

***

My father is whom I thought of when I thought of a Bosnian man. Not my friends from high school who seemed too young still, flippant and impractical, and not their fathers, who had eagerness in their eyes where there should've been regret. I didn't think of myself, because man and Bosnian were only approximations of my reality.

He came to all my elementary school recitals, to all the baseball games when I played for the middle school team, even though he didn't like sports, much less baseball; he taught me to swim, to ride a bike, to multiply; he taught me that only male seahorses give birth and only female mosquitoes bite, that you measure the size of a country not by its area, but its population. He was quick and capable, with a manly ingenuity about him. He could take things apart and put them back together, and I envied him and didn't care.

My father counted down the days until his return to Bosnia. He moved furniture, drove a truck for a time, painted houses with his brother and packed medicine at a pharmaceutical company, making it to the front office eventually—and all the while he counted down the days. Weekends, he went to Mostar, one of the Bosnian cafés on Gravois, and he sat there drinking his cappuccino and counting down the days. I can picture him well, a corner table man, rocking gently in the chair to the music, a raised knee in his interlocked hands, a man lonely and distracted in his joy of the moment. His future was in his past, and patience and regret were the heart and soul of his disposition.

He'd come into my room to drop off the mail and he'd ask, How was the party last night? or, Were there any girls at the pool? He asked with a sated little half-grin he couldn't pull off, the meaning behind the smile as unreachable for him as it was for me.

                                   ***

Nina and I let the blue smoke fill our silence, until that too was gone. She was looking at me, on her back now, our sides touching. Something slow and mocking about that look, or maybe it was in the lines of kohl with the little flick above the outer edge of her lashes. Maybe in the subtle arch of her brows. Gone with the smoke was the curious stare she was giving me before, hard-eyed, her mouth halfway smirking, looking at me like I was an interesting challenge. That was something I never wanted her to see in me.

"Please. I need you there."

"Trust me, Nina, you don't."

She turned on her stomach, letting her chin rest on my chest, her face collapsed into a pout. I put a pillow under my head to better see what she was doing. We became silent again because there was nothing more to say, though it felt more deliberate than that at the moment. She moved up toward me, slowly and without words, her body sliding over mine. Then she pressed her mouth against my lower lip, kissing me. My mouth slackened under hers, relented to it, played along like a wall plays along. She was kissing me with a hard, heedless plunge of her tongue, her hips grinding against my motionless bulk. My arms were too limp to push against her dipping shoulders, slack and defenseless. I felt a double beat inside my chest, a ropey tightness.

Suddenly, she was standing by the bed, taking off her clothes with an unthinking swiftness, undressing down to her bra and panties. Before I could speak, she was on top of me again, tugging at my shorts. The ash spilled onto the sheets like a horrible parody. Telling her the truth now seemed further from possible than it had ever been, and anything else I could've said to stop it would've been a lie she'd recognize and interpret in ways that'd hurt her more than this would hurt her—or so I thought, closing my eyes and letting her pull at my clothes.

***

It was my mother I worried about. My mother who grilled me about the lack of girls in my life. My mother who dreamed out loud about a daughter-in-law and grandchildren. My mother who made me nervous when she looked at me tight-eyed and frowning, leaning forward on the sofa we shared, her arms crossed over her knees. I knew she thought I was strange and I feared that the question of why I was that way would eventually find homosexuality as the answer. I could see the question formulating in her mind whenever her eyes narrowed and her mouth became a compact, opaque little frown.

She'd been a civil engineer in Bosnia, but in Germany took care of an old wealthy couple and an even older and wealthier widow. The state provided money for groceries and rent and so my mother really worked for life after Germany, for the right to decide where that life would take place. Not Bosnia, because there was no future there for her only child. I came to America for you, she'd say when she needed to prove her love or have me prove mine—and I'd only think about the disappointment that awaited her.

Now my betrayal was double-edged; by dating Nina I was making my mother hopeful and impatient. Nina and I had dinners at each other's house, with each other's family, and the talk was always ambitious and sweet, especially when my mother was at the head of the table, with wedding dates and children's names spoken over bell peppers and roasted potatoes. Nina helped my mother cook while listening to her stories and relieving her momentarily of the pain and loneliness of a daughterless existence, the strange nature of her only son.

⁂

Rumors spread quickly in high school; by the first day of senior year all the Bosnians knew about Nina and me, the eyes of the boys narrowed and mouths grinning in congratulation. They said they'd suspected something was going on. It was excruciating, their happy suspicions. The girls weren't surprised either—they'd seen it coming.

I walked Nina to her classes, hand in hand down busy hallways, and we sat close together at lunch in the Bosnian corner, her thigh rubbing against mine under the table. Part of me became content with this arrangement, this fantasy of us. I started to take a lulling comfort in our public tenderness, our ceremony of heterosexual love. For the first time in my life I wasn't scared of being found out because for the first time I was sure I was fooling everybody. But guilt brought me back to reality each time, the thought of my silent partner in this deception, the friend I was betraying for an illusion of freedom.

We went to nightclubs because she wanted to. We danced under the boozy lights to blurred music. We went to parties and she mingled while I kept to the edges of rooms, sober and bored. We fought lightly, got jealous for no good reason, said bitter things we did not mean, played all the sly and dismal games boys and girls play when they think they are men and women. We had the backseat tit for tat in random parking lots for the sake of excitement and risk. We went down on each other with our clever hands and mouths and our pleasure was fleeting and incomplete.

Nina cooked for me sometimes, tender and fussy in her mother's apron, sprinkling salt through the bunched tips of her fingers. I looked in now and then, standing under the archway to the kitchen, shy, anxious, and incredibly moved.

Whenever Nina said she loved me, I felt a complicated pity for us both, and then I said it back.

***

The Dollhouse was a small, ramshackle record store on Tesson Ferry I visited regularly looking for used CDs. "Only Shallow" slithered out of the wall-mounted speakers as I made my way to the ambiguously titled Rock section, nodding at Dave behind the counter. I was looking for The Smiths' first album, which Nina had borrowed and subsequently lost. As I browsed without luck, I noticed a boy with a familiar face doing the same across the aisle of shelves. It was a good face, with a muscular curve to the cheekbones and gently slanted eyes. A face wasted on a boy, my mother would say. I was sure I knew him from high school, but his name wouldn't come to me. I moved around to his side, wanted to brush his shoulder against mine. Instead I picked out some random CD and pretended to look at it. He wore a buttoned long-sleeve shirt, heavy for spring, khakis, and tan sneakers. He held two Miles Davis CDs in each hand like he was weighing them on a scale. With a sudden grace his name came to me.

We talked a long time, Ryan and I. It was effortless. I don't remember any subject in detail because we didn't stay on one for long. He was majoring in English at Webster, where I'd just gotten accepted. We talked about that. We talked about high school, the film class we had had together. We talked about the songs in The Dollhouse, how each song changed the room's feel. He had a way of staring off to the side, looking at my shoulder rather than my face.

"What're you looking for?"

"Miles Davis, if I can make a decision."

"You're into jazz?"

"Actually, my ex-girlfriend, she listened to him a lot when we were together, so I had to listen to him. A lot. You know how it is." I nodded, smiling, and wondered if I did know. "It grew on me. Only problem is I don't know which one to buy." He looked sadly at both. "What do you think I should do?"

I wished I had an answer for him, but everything I know about jazz I learned afterwards, in preparation for next time, our second chance encounter.

I was walking toward my car when I suddenly turned around and went back to The Dollhouse. I stood by the store window inclined and motionless, peeking in through a narrow gap between two posters. Ryan had only one CD in his hand now. He took it out of its case, then looked around indifferently. Dave was on the phone, his elbow propped on the counter, his head in his palm, eyes on the floor; there was only one other customer, a hip-swinging girl with headphones on and her back to everybody. Ryan moved toward an empty corner and farther away. I pressed my face against the glass. He looked around some more while his hand moved to his breast pocket. He slipped the CD in—and it was gone. I'd seen it coming, the minute gesture of it, yet it astonished me. I thought how charming, what a beautiful and charming thing it was, caught by my eyes alone, I'd hold it forever in my heart.

***

The more times Nina and I had sex, the more receptive I became, the more I learned to tune my mind out and let my body follow the rhythm of hers. I never kept my eyes open too long, though, never said a word. I trembled without being eager. And sometimes I lost my erection, which happened as naturally as a moan during orgasm, though there was as little embarrassment for me in the one as there was passion in the other. Afterwards, elbow cupped in palm, smoking a cigarette, she'd tell me that it happens. It's all right, she'd say. We're getting there. All I wanted then was to drop at her feet and beg for all the forgiveness in her soul.

***

Before we parted at The Dollhouse, Ryan casually mentioned he'd be at a small club off Lindbergh on Friday. It felt like an invitation to a chance meeting. I brought Nina along in case he didn't show. But he was there, in a corner booth with some blond, a friend of his. Nina and the girl made fast friends and had long, shouting conversations over the music. Ryan charmed the waitresses with his ambiguous smile. I watched people in the club, making comments to the table when it became too irresistible. There was a revolving door of local bands, with girls and boys wriggling on the dance floor below the stage or stoically wasted at the bar, staring into the distance like castaways. Ryan got a kick out of my fake ID, turned it over in his hand, compared it to his own, said mine felt more like the real thing.

We kept meeting, sometimes alone, sometimes not. And I kept noticing how his eyes never met mine in conversation, how his slow and indirect way of looking at me allowed for varied interpretations, for tenderness and detachment. I felt a hesitant, guarded attraction toward him, giving him the corner-of-the-eye leer I had perfected by necessity in high school. There was the old buzzing in my limbs whenever he was near, a sharp murmur in my bones that turned my body into a coded message. I thought of him during sex with Nina and the stillness that came after, when the rare screech of faraway tires was the only sound in the night and my dreams.

I graduated high school and enrolled at Webster, impulsively choosing Art History as my major. I read large books with glossy pictures and began to see analogies in real life, flesh and blood metaphors wherever I looked. I saw Ryan in Bronzino's *Portrait of a Young Man*, in the long slope of the nose and small, hard mouth, the noble cheekbones. Saw my mother rigid, marble-poised, an Assyrian statue. And Nina, when she was lost in thought, legs folded under her on the sofa, looking out of the window at the rain, past the rain, silver and sudden—she had something of the Madonna in Byzantine mosaics in her doomed and ethereal gaze.

And where was I in all this? Buried in grays and greens, misshapen and gaping, Saturn devouring his children.

***

Nina didn't go to community college like she'd promised her parents, even when the spring semester came around. Instead she started working full-time at her job, selling tickets at the Ronnie's multiplex on Lindbergh. She worked weekends, too, and I took every opportunity to see Ryan on those busy Fridays or Saturdays. We went to a tavern not far from campus. Students from both of our departments hung out there, sitting around oak tables under Cardinals pennants and signed pictures of ballplayers, the smell of fried potatoes coming from the noisy kitchen. Despite the large group, I talked without censoring my words or concealing my gestures. I felt lighthearted and invulnerable, at a point of safe arrival. I felt I was finally with people for whom my sexuality would be at the very edge of their perception of me.

Ryan and I usually stayed until closing time, and afterwards, not yet tired but with nowhere to go, we just drove around South County in his red Camaro, music seeping in and out of the open windows. Traffic would be sparse, the traffic lights blinking yellow, raw asphalt and dark sky filling up the windshield. We drove into downtown sometimes, its streets geometric and empty, then back south on Highway 55, along the Mississippi. Sometimes we drove into the Bosnian area in South City, that stretch of Gravois before and after it intersects with Morganford. Benevolent Ryan never asked any questions. And sometimes we drove over the bridge into Illinois instead, with visions of Chicago under a starlit night. Once, after we'd just seen the skeleton frames of another Camaro in front of some rundown house in South County, Ryan said that these nowhere drives inspired him like nothing else. He was tipsy, one careless hand on the steering wheel, the other gesturing toward the dark, pointing out a dingo pack of young boys huddled on the street corner, trying to map out, he said, the shortest route toward their desires.

I had done these nowhere drives before, with the Bosnians, but now was different, a purer mixture of adrenaline and the dark, with more poetry to the night, an element of fate that didn't depend on the outcome for its meaning. Ryan challenged other cars at stoplights, pressing down on the gas pedal while in park only to feel the promise of acceleration, the tremble of the frame. When the light flashed green, we watched the other car roar forward, marking the pavement black, the hot screech of its tires deafening out against the night sky. The music we played now was no longer just a taunting announcement of our presence, like the defiant rap from high school, but an evocation of deeper wants, an attempt to communicate secrets, a more sincere and subtle expression of our wonder and unapologetic joy. We played *Meat is Murder* and *Louder Than Bombs*. The music never rose above our voices; we never had to turn it down to be heard.

Our nights usually ended around Grant's Farm, the car parked on the grass at the side of the road, serving only as a radio now, and Ryan and I sitting on a wooden fence that gave out on a field, beyond it a small forest, the trees turned to silhouettes in the moonlight. There was a deep-breathing calm to late nights in winter, even without snow, even in a city like St. Louis. We sat on the fence in silence, listening to music and the phantom gallop of the horses that ran there during the day. I could tell Ryan was sober again when he stopped looking me in the eyes.

***

She was peeling a grapefruit, wearing a summer dress, the lilac faded from too many washes, and didn't have any make-up on. She sat in the armchair in my room, legs crossed, one of the worn-out slippers my mother had given her tilting on the brink of her suspended foot. The white slippers had turned a buttery yellow around the edges. My mother had given them to her so her feet wouldn't get cold. It was May.

I sat on the bed with a book spread out in front of me, studying for my last exam of the school year. The fan was working. We were silent. The sun shone behind drawn curtains, and the air was charged with a secret resolution that I wouldn't have the courage to follow through for yet another day. For her it probably just smelled of citrus. I was looking at paintings trying to memorize their names, the names of their makers, dates and certain techniques, but thought instead about how coming out to

Nina was to signal a new beginning, a new life, that it still would, but not for the better. I thought about my mother when I heard her laughing, watching sitcoms in the living room. I thought about my father's silence, then my own.

In that respect, it was like any other day.

She shifted her weight in the armchair and I looked up. With one flick of her foot, the slipper came flying at my head. I caught it by the heel, pretended to rip off the puff, then threw it aside. She pierced a slice of grapefruit between her teeth, took it up on her tongue to crush the juices out against the roof of her mouth. I smiled, she smiled—and that was as far as it went.

***

Nina complained of a headache and left. I thought about calling Ryan as I gathered up the grapefruit peel she had scattered on the table, the skin still pungent, evocative of what was lost. I thought better of it and drove out to his apartment.

Ryan lived by himself in a rugged but trendy neighborhood off Manchester, in an apartment on the fifth floor. He opened the door in a sweat-drenched T-shirt, said he just got back from a run. Clothing was strewn on the carpet and over furniture, paintings on the wall, one by a former girlfriend, an abstract thing, cubes and flames. The room smelled of soul food from the restaurant below. While he showered I looked over his books, though I knew them all, had figured out which ones were by gay authors. I took out a collection by Hart Crane, leafed through it leaning against the bookshelf. My favorite vision of Ryan was in the white-fenced garden behind the library at Webster, slouching on a hard bench under a speckled shade with a book in his lap and a pencil behind his ear. The water turned off and I pictured him now in front of the damp mirror, his face slurred by the steam on the glass. I put the book back.

The window was open, the sky orange with sunset. On the roof of the building across the street were two plastic recliners like the kind you'd see at a pool, one beige and the other white. Ryan joined me by the window, barefoot in dark jeans, wearing a gray shirt with the name of our college arched over his chest. I could tell he'd just shaved by the tentative blue sheen on his cheek, the bit of crimson on the base of his jaw.

"There's this couple and they suntan up there," he said, gesturing toward the rooftop with his chin.

We sat down on the couch trying to figure out what to do with the night. He sat a cushion away, slouching slightly, one foot against the edge of the table. He was talking about the movies.

"It's too early for the movies," I said. "Plus she's not working tonight."

"I don't mind paying."

I felt reckless and brave. "Except for CDs, right?"

He turned toward me with an almost mocking slowness, the tight smile already on his lips. I shifted my body to face him and we were silent.

"What do you want me to say?"

"Nothing, I guess. I just want you to know that I know."

His stare became vague again, gentle with obliqueness. He stopped smiling. I touched his face and he closed his eyes. We kissed.

On the way to the bedroom, I gripped him by his pale biceps and pressed him against the doorjamb. We kissed harder. He tasted of cherries and soft wax. He tipped his chin; his throat was humid and smooth. I was taller than him; it gave me confidence. He palmed my crotch and I clenched his hair. He bit my lip and I bit back. His bed was a couple of mattresses stacked on top of one another. I pulled him down on it by his hips.

We jerked each other off with a certain clumsiness that put us both at ease, I think. Ryan began to talk about our plans again like nothing had happened, or like whatever had happened was now over. It angered and relieved me. A violet-blue dusk filled the window, half-open to the rumble of trucks, the jagged siren of an ambulance. Ryan lay with his head in the crook of my arm, naked above the waist, pale and delicately muscled. His nipples were dark, small towers. He talked and clawed at his arm, bumpy with mosquito bites, scarlet-tipped, little mounds I brushed my stubbled cheek against when he wasn't expecting it.

***

Part of my job with the Census was to help set up block parties in neighborhoods with low participation rates, where people did not fill out the form that came in the mail. These were in predominantly minority neighborhoods. Our supervisor said it was fear more than laziness, a deep suspicion and fear. The block parties I set up to promote the Census in the Bevo Mill area were a failure in the sense that no Bosnians ever showed up to them, forcing me to go to the nearest bars and try to persuade the bemused patrons there to come, worried always that beneath their disinterest there lurked a hint of ridicule and hate. *Peder* is the word for gay in the Bosnian language and it's almost impossible to say without sounding like an insult, because it means both homosexual and fag, because for us there's no difference. I listened for this word in the white noise of the crowd, against the foreign blare of the music, but when I heard it, or thought I did, I never had the guts to turn my head, to stare back with the pride of the unwounded.

***

I told my parents as soon as I came home from Ryan's. My mother cried in a hushed way, her head bowing into the tissues she held; my father only looked at me with that heavy patience in his eyes, abstractly holding his reading glasses. I knew that for the rest of my life I'd have to explain myself to them and thought it was the least I could do. Later, my mother came to my bedside, and I remember how she tried to shape the words with her lips but made no sound louder than a whisper, each word bulky with meaning. How, as she sat straight-backed on the edge of my bed, with her ruddy hands clasped in her lap, her sad, softly inquisitive eyes, she looked like a woman in a painting I'd never seen but was sure existed.

Emil, she said, you understand that there is more than love? She could make you very happy. Nina, she said, is a good girl. From the lighted hallway, only a voice, my father called her name, told her to leave the boy alone. She got up and simply closed the door. She came back and sat down again. I turned on the bedside table lamp without moving my head off the pillow. Her shadow appeared against the far wall, a woman older than her, bundled in black. She began repeating herself, love and happiness, how they are not the same, and I said, I know, sadly, tenderly, I know, like hushing a child. I remember the gray where her hair parted when she bent down to muffle her sobs against my chest.

***

I told Nina the first chance we were alone, coming to pick her up for a party we'd never get to. I held her by the elbows and tried to look into her eyes as I said it. She seemed to stop listening as soon as she realized what I was saying. She yelled and cried and beat against me with her small fists. She called me a pervert and a freak. Ryan, she said, as though she knew, and I felt the dizzy heat of a blush. Ryan, she said bitterly. Then she calmed, sitting with her knees together and ankles apart, still wearing the indigo bathrobe I'd found her in. It hung open down the middle, revealing the apricot of her chest and belly. I wanted to go over to the sofa and comfort her, but didn't think I had the right. She was staring out into nothing, with that almost serene and utterly fragile look on her face, the make-up around her eyes runny from tears.

I tried to reason with Nina in the following days, to apologize, to tell her that I loved her and always would; I called her on the phone repeatedly, but she either wouldn't answer or she'd curse at me in a small but savage voice before hanging up. I drove to her home, but it was her mother who kept coming to the door, turning me away each time with lessening affection. Finally, I went to Nina's work and asked for her forgiveness through the little hole at the ticket counter, but she only said she'd call security if I didn't leave. I reached my arm inside and she jerked back like it was a snake, her mouth ragged with disgust behind the streaked glass.

One day my mother told me that one of her friends came by for coffee and asked her about me, my disease, as the woman had called it, *bolest*. I'd have laughed at this if I didn't think my mother secretly felt the same way. I'd have laughed if I didn't know that Nina had told.

It felt like the longest summer of my life. By the end of it, Ryan and I had fizzled out. I cannot think of a more careless yet fitting expression than that. I'd been pretending to my parents that I was taking a summer class in Chemistry just to see him, staying at his apartment every weekday from eleven to two, then every other day, and then I just walked the South County mall trying to fill the time. I told everybody in our group that I was gay, but I never told them that Ryan was my lover. I sensed he wanted our relationship to be kept a secret. We always had an instinct for each other's needs, understood the subtext of each other's body language. I knew what he wanted and gave it to him because it was what I had wanted too, at first, because it had been easy to give. Then I wanted to give more and knew he would never give as much in return. The last time we made love was hasty and intense. It felt like the last time.

***

If the Census Bureau were to relocate me tomorrow, there wouldn't be any heartbreak on my part. The sweet molasses smell of baklava never reminded me of coppersmith huts lining cobbled streets, or old Ottoman bridges like the one in the painting that hung in Café Mostar. My earliest childhood recollections are not of the Bosnian city I was born in, but of a small town in the south of Germany, its blue-roofed tower, its old men with El Greco expressions sitting outside of the ice cream parlor. After those memories comes only the whitewash of St. Louis.

I was in Café Mostar today asking the owner if I could leave some Census pamphlets off with him when I saw Nina through a crowd of broad shoulders and unshaven faces. She was sitting with a group of young men near the billiards table in the back. She held on to the arm of a dark-haired, handsome boy, talking over his shoulder and gesturing with a cigarette in her free hand. I couldn't even imagine going over to her through the maze of tables, saying hello, how've you been. I just watched her out of the corner of my eye, another familiar-looking stranger from where she sat—from where I sat, from where we both sat—in a room full of familiar-looking strangers. She seemed happy, forgetful, and I'd like to think it was out of love, not fear, that I didn't approach her. She wore knee-high boots and light green shorts barely visible beneath an oversized jersey. It was the all-white home uniform of the Bosnian national soccer team, the number ten shirt, too big for her and probably his. She did seem happy.

Like Coming Home

When Daniel thought of his father—while watching from his bleak little cubicle the chair the unsmiling secretary had just deserted, or awake at night, with the after-rain drip and gurgle outside of his window, the wet gleam of sidewalk and moon— he thought of his father's peculiar means of making money as a young man, smuggling blue jeans from Italy to Yugoslavia. (Ah, the bright, ephemeral, counterfeit nature of borders and border crossers.)

Daniel's father did his buying in Trieste, and the particular market his father had gone to was a five-minute walk from where Daniel sat now, the Miramare Café. It still sold jeans among its glossy fruits and vegetables, and if Daniel had bought a pair as he walked by the overflowing wooden stalls earlier, he would have fulfilled the main purpose of his visit to Trieste. But then he would have had to tour the rest of the city with a bag in his hand. His father carried up to five bags at one time, but his excursions were limited: he came, did his business, and left. Daniel was aware of early events in his father's life by the stories his mother told him in a poignantly longwinded way. The rest he imagined.

The Miramare, named after the whitewashed castle on the Gulf of Trieste—where a phony empress had gone genuinely mad from wild mourning for her shipwrecked husband, or so I've read—was a seaside café with polished windows, a creaking door, a creamy terrace with only three tables, and a horizon-inducing view of the dusky blue Adriatic. (Had he been more artistically inclined, he would have thought the water a nostalgic blue, the horizon a scarlet slit athwart the violet and orange wound of sunset.) A couple of large gulls glided across the sea, making gull sounds and casting gull-shaped, dimly glimmering shadows over the water. Daniel could also see a good stretch of the pale stone esplanade before it curved and disappeared behind red-roofed houses, and farther down, the moored boats in the blue marina, farther still, the boats at sea, sails flapping like flags of surrender.

Oh, the poetry of port towns.

Daniel, brown-haired, broad-shouldered, and almost twenty-four, sat at the center table, leaning gently to one side in his chair. The table behind him was empty. At the table facing him sat a long-limbed blond in a clinging lilac dress. She was reading the *Duino Elegies*, which Rilke had written at a different castle near Trieste. (Trieste was swarming with ghosts, his guide book said.) Pretending to read the dessert section of the menu—cakes sonorously named after Renaissance sculptors and painters—Daniel stared at the girl, shamelessly eavesdropping on the conversation she was having with the waiter, a lithe, acne-scarred, handsome boy, wearing his dark hair slicked back in the preferred style of Italian waiters. Daniel felt no shame because he could not understand what they were saying, though it all sounded dimly poetic to him. (The girl was asking in careful, school-learned Italian, with Slavic tints and overtones, when the last train for Venice was leaving, and the boy put down his empty tray—a dark, circular, raised-rim tray, streaked with moisture—and stroked his red-stippled chin, before saying he wasn't sure.)

The door creaked and they were alone. The girl took a small sip of her latté—a tickle between porcelain and lip—and went back to her book, slouching forward, her elbows on the table, the book held awkwardly in one hand, licking the index of the other to turn the page. Daniel's Italian consisted of a few touristy phrases provided by his guide book, not nearly enough to attempt a coherent conversation with this girl, whose thick lulling lips sometimes tenderly mouthed the words on the page, brows lowered, and swift eyes narrowed as she read. Daniel wanted to talk to her, or at least offer a clever, echoing aside that would hint at the ghost of a romance. His father had met his mother in Trieste.

As the story goes, his father, bags in hand, heading for the train station, saw Daniel's mother, who was vacationing in Italy, sitting in a café. He sat down across from her for the sole purpose of gazing at her foreign beauty. After exchanging glances, he went over to her table, but because each thought that the other was actually Italian, and since their combined knowledge of the language amounted to a half-dozen words, neither attempted a conversation, and their communication by gestures soon floundered. So they sat in silence until his father muttered something in Serbo-Croatian—he had banged his knee against the table and cursed—and the whole misunderstanding was cleared up.

Then the smoldering romance began, and they ended up spending the entire day together promising to meet again as they parted on the train platform. Here his mother liked to go into great detail, positioning herself on the edge of the platform, misty-eyed, clutching a tissue, while his father, one foot aboard the train, shouted something inspired and unforgettable—which she did not hear—as it took him into the convenient sunset. And here Daniel would object, accusing his mother of confusing her life with a romantic novel. But she stood by her story, though he believed that what she had described was a fantastic scene that never was and could never be reenacted in reality, no matter how ardently his mother desired to play the part.

Daniel took out of his pocket a silver wristwatch with a square face and black leather band that used to belong to his father. Despite its handcuff feel, he cherished it as a simple reminder of what he had lost. He put the watch on the table next to his half-eaten Verrocchio. "*Il conto, grazie*," he called out self-consciously to the reappeared waiter after calculating he would have only twenty minutes or so to buy the jeans and get to Trieste Centrale, where *his* train was waiting. The smile on the young waiter's face when he saw Daniel's tip seemed genuine and he showed his appreciation with a hearty, accented "Thank you." Daniel looked at the girl as she leaned back in her chair, the book sprawled on her lap, and made up his mind to casually praise Rilke (the poet of thresholds and doors) as he passed by her table. (He did not notice the legs of the chair she so languorously sat in reflected against the pale yellow cement, or how the colors of sunset shone and swam in the palm trees that lined one side of the esplanade, nor did he hear the exuberant buzzing of a bee that circled a plotted plant in the corner of the terrace—or else he confused it with the noise in his heart.) Daniel rose suddenly, approached slowly, cleared his throat loudly—and she looked up. He opened his mouth, caught the blue dazzle of her eyes, and was struck dumb. Out on the street, he cursed his cowardliness in all the languages he spoke, with all the blunt fluency of regret.

Now, the word digression has for me a physical quality: a young man, walking toward the main square of a European city, is abruptly seduced by the optical siren song of some scrawny, vivid alley snaking its ancient way uphill; he can see the great church tower with its rust-colored, aesthetically cracked bell— and what's more the heat is becoming oppressive, the sunlight glinting off the pawn-shaped, black-domed automobile barriers in town—but he turns, he digresses, he sins into the alley anyway, drawn by curiosity and a vague longing for beauty, by the luminous knick-knacks in a teeming shop, the bargaining tongues of shopkeepers, the chance sight, atop some fancy ironwork balcony, of a Madonna in a sundress or accidental Juliet hanging her linens, graceful legs shimmering through the gaps in the flowering balustrade.

Daniel was not such a young man. He only grew digressive with age.

No, he was not such a young man and made it to the Piazza dell'Unita d'Italia in no time. He began looking for stores that sold jeans. It was a bit nauseating in the dense hot crowd of the wide square, under the stone-eyed Habsburg Emperors and their horses (rigid and rearing, respectively), surrounded by architecture nostalgic for the foundation of an empire. (Trieste suffers under the charming spell of an identity crisis, with its imposing German architecture and voluptuous Italian people, and its out-of-the-way graffiti, on bridges and in tunnels, proclaiming the city as Slovenian.) Daniel got onto a street that branched out of the square, passing up several inviting storefronts. Two old men sat on the curved steps of a residential building, playing chess with gloomy concentration. Young boys grunted and screamed as they passed a ball back and forth in a narrow side street, while girls, watching from the sidewalk, seemed unable to take their passion seriously. But they looked intrigued, hands shielding their lips as they gossiped and burst into laughter. In their pink and orange skirts, taken for granted by the young boys and old men, they lived only for the leer of a foreigner, or so Daniel liked to imagine. He knew better. They were not interested in him despite the white-toothed smiles and the sly look in their eyes. They were not interested, but they appeared to be. That was their charm.

"*Signor,*" a voice cried out behind him—light-filled and achingly soft—and Daniel, though he did not think he was being called, turned around to marry the senses. He turned too suddenly, and she bumped into him with her delicate shoulder. Her smile was slight and lovely. Opening her fist, she revealed a familiar-looking wristwatch coiled in her smooth golden palm. Instinctively, Daniel reached into his pocket and found nothing.

"*Grazie,*" he said. He wanted to say more. She seemed to know it, too, inclining her blond head to one side and looking up at him with those eyes. But he only repeated his thanks and stared back at her, hoping that his eyes could express what his lack of Italian kept him from saying. It would be an awkward parting.

***

I scrambled up the basement stairs, peeked into the kitchen through the open door, then closed it. I would have locked it, too, if it had a lock. Sabina lay on the yellow and black striped sofa, covered up to her milky neck in a chocolate blanket to create the successful illusion of nakedness underneath. I straddled her legs, careful not to hurt the brittle things under my weight, and lowered my head to place a cautious kiss on the smooth spot between her brows. I straightened up to see what effect this initial, light contact had on her. It had not melted the iciness of her pale face, but there was a hint of tenderness in her big, dark eyes. I daringly proceeded to kiss her forehead, nose, and both cheeks. My hands trembled and my heart thumped as I pressed my lips against her silky, closed mouth, initiating our first kiss.

The kissing session went on uninterrupted in the relative safety of the semi-dark basement. I was aware that she accepted my kisses without seeking them, and that she kissed me back without anticipation, but I didn't care. Accidentally, I got her to laugh when I kissed her milky-white and apparently ticklish throat, and when I, spurred on by a harmless obsession, licked her left earlobe, I was awarded with seeing her entire ear turn a torrid red. Yet, she was bored, but the thrill of discovery reduced the tormenting effect her sullen boredom usually had on me. So I continued kissing her, because she let me. She let me throw the blanket on the floor, let me grasp her knees and gently part her legs, but when my hands started traveling up her excitingly warm thighs she suddenly claimed hearing a noise from the stairs, and her legs snapped shut like a bear trap.

I ran to the stairs, saw nothing, rushed back, and was shocked by the disturbing reappearance of the dark blanket, draped over her body. I sat down on the edge of the sofa, my desire hushed. Sabina touched my arm with her cool toes, but I did not react. I just stared at my feet, amazed by how, if I kept my eyes down, I could convince myself that nobody else in the world existed. I still liked her though, and knew, even then, at the age of thirteen, that I always would. I even liked the embarrassment caused by her making me admit that I did. I liked her the way I liked music, instinctively and devotedly, and, like with music, I didn't know when I started liking her, because I did not know a time when I didn't. She liked me, too, I was certain of that, though I would purposely doubt it so to make the eventual reassurance all the more pleasurable.

Sabina got up and walked barefoot across the floor to turn on the small radio. Her hips swaying to a beat-heavy song, she fondled the volume button, then began changing the station—hips still swaying—until she found a slow song she liked. She offered me her creamy, red-nailed hand, and I took it without hesitation. We pressed our cheeks together and turned in a circle. She kept stepping on my foot, but I did not say anything. She was too beautiful not be a little clumsy, and I could not open my mouth anyway. Inhaling the kitchen scent of her shiny black hair—she had helped prepare breakfast—I was overwhelmed with a feeling of voluptuous happiness and vague anguish, which left me speechless. The romantic lyrics of the song proved incredibly inadequate in mirroring my emotions—but the melody said all I felt.

I slowed our twirling and was about to dampen the bare part of her shoulder with a kiss when the music suddenly stopped. My mother pointed up toward the door. Sabina, blushing, ran upstairs; I wanted to run but was frozen by the severe stare of my mother. She viewed the games we played in the basement with motherly worry and mild disgust, which made me feel ashamed (which I suspected was the purpose). It made me angry, too. Sometimes it seemed that my mother only existed to deny my every satisfaction.

A dark figure had appeared in the lighted doorway; coming down the stairs it took the shape of my father. There was a smile on his face that I knew was meant for me only, because when my mother turned, it disappeared.

***

The window on the train from Trieste to Zagreb was aflame with sundown. Daniel dozed off with his head resting against the thick glass. There was a constant promise of color—an oblique burst of aquamarine, a streak of azure flashing at the shoulder—that diffused into sudden gray at every turn of the dreaming eye. He saw long legs crossing and uncrossing beneath a table in continuous motion, while his father gestured from an incidental angle, moving his lips in vain. White-shirted and wearing black pants, not himself at all in appearance, but his father under the authority of dream logic, he was later checking Daniel's boarding pass in a train cabin that resembled the inside of a small, unpleasant bar Daniel had visited on his twenty-first birthday. Then, his father a mere bystander again, a younger version of Daniel made his way through a crowd at a beach toward a raised, swanlike arm in the gray distance. And from this labyrinth of meaning, this offhand riddle, Daniel awoke with only splinters of lucid recollection.

Across the Zagreb Kolodvor, a columned, neoclassical building, a Hungarian's dream, is a finely manicured park with a fountain in the center and an equestrian statue on its southern edge, facing the elongated station—but Daniel was already in the taxi, looking sullenly out of the glare-smudged window, distracted by inner landmarks. On the bus to Split, a smooth highway run, he fell asleep again, awoke, changed buses in the city Diocletian had built, and was on his way to Mostar. It had been humid and grimy in Split, the bus station shoddy and loud, the sun a blind menace, the sea a blue mirage. Daniel was glad to board the bus. But soon the titillating coast was gone: the hoary, green-veined, precipitous rocks, the blue-pebbled beaches, the sea's lacy, tattered foam hem; and the air-conditioning died with an abrupt, thorny rustle; and the dry inland wind brought only the briefest relief; and the bus was ponderous; and it stopped at every sea-forsaken little village to pick up a ghostly swirl of silver dust on the ground, or a musing white goat in the adjacent pasture; and it was all so maddening and hot and slow; and the border was jammed, and the border was close, and the border was far away.

He fell asleep once more, a hot, wet dreamless wink of time. When he awoke, he looked out of the window and instantly realized where he was. (It was not really knowledge, but a deep feeling, let's call it an articulate chill along the spine or the loud moan of intuition.) He asked the driver if another bus was coming and exited at the nearest stop, slightly hunching under his backpack and swinging his bag with the fire engine red of the Levi's logo on it. The gate was thin and black, one harp-shaped door ajar, as if held open for Daniel by some ghostly porter.

The cemetery in Mostar was sprawling and endless. So it seemed to Daniel as he searched for his father's grave among the tooth-shaped stones, the marble gleaming blue in the mounting dusk. Walking through it, Daniel was pleasantly surprised to feel the same rush of fear he had known from his childhood wanderings through cemeteries, when, dared by a friend to walk from one end to the other with only the trembling moon as accompaniment, he instead ran down the nimble pavement, his heart beating in his ear, as soon as he was sure the winding path had taken him out of view. (I was never really sure, but eventually, at a small sound that blossomed into a roar even my booming heartbeat could not drown out—a long-echoing twig snap, or the wind-magnified crackle of autumn leaves— the terror of ridicule and hazing would be instantly overcome by the more pressing, merciless terror of darkness and the unknown.) The fear and excitement faded quickly, though, and Daniel became impatient, walking toward the cemetery's vague southwest corner, where his mother had told him his father was buried.

When he finally reached his father's white headstone, his name written in curling bronze, all Daniel could do was stare at it. He stared at the name and the stone, the even pile of dirt, suddenly feeling as though he had come to this cemetery by mistake, by a wrongly given direction, and was now standing over the grave of some random stranger. (How could *my* father be *here*?) Yet he kept staring. He had come here to learn something about his father that his mother's stories could not teach him. To resolve in one elegant stroke the whole mystery of his father's life. Now Daniel realized he could never complete such a task, nor could he abandon it.

When she had heard of his father's death, his mother returned to Bosnia to bury him, while Daniel stayed in Croatia, waiting for her, and somehow his, return. A few days after coming back, his mother told him with tears in her eyes, and without him asking, that his father had died by stepping on a landmine. What side planted the landmine mattered as little to his mother then as it did to Daniel now, and to know would only further complicate his already complicated sense of resentment. His father was a patriot even at the worst of times, an optimist despite being Bosnian. He had taught him to respect Muslims and Christians before Daniel became aware of their differences, and Daniel remembered once overhearing his father say that taking sides in a war meant defending the bad against the worse. He remembered those words not because they were right—they weren't, not in this war—but because he had taken them seriously when he first heard them. Now they were the only words of his father he remembered.

Daniel stood over the grave for a while longer, then sat down on the concrete, spreading his legs out over the grass. The sun was setting behind blurred hills, orange and purple, silky and rough-edged, its motley iridescence trembling on an anonymous leaf. The fragrant golden lilies shook their heads in the wind. Daniel thought in the simplest of terms: what if his father were here right now, free of all temporal and spatial restraints, standing right there, looking over him, and looking into him, his past and future, his memories and desires, as sullen and restless as his son. There appeared a faint new moon in the moist violet of the night sky. The wind still sang in the bushes, delicate, discreet, able to shiver a rose petal, make a skirt on the clothesline bloom, shut a door in an empty room, the draft of otherworldliness that runs through our everyday lives.

***

Sabina stood looking out at the sea, her hands at her side, one leg slightly bent. I was fascinated with the dip of her back, with the beauty of her pose. She wore an orange dress, its straps sliding off her shoulders. The waves washed over her feet before retreating, then surged forward again. She bent down to bathe her hands in the blue water. I did not like her anymore. What I felt for her now was stronger and more mysterious.

I threw a pebble into the sea to hear the plop; it was a sound akin to a tongue click. I picked up another, but let it fall from my hand to cover a yawn. Sabina yawned too, raising her arms above her head, revealing the peach-colored hollow of her armpit, and reaching skyward with her spread fingers. She resumed her gazing, hands clasped behind her nape, a pretty frown on her face. I wondered what she was thinking but did not dare ask. She would either answer with distracted simplicity, which I no longer found charming, or with complete indifference, which I hated. I didn't even really care. All I wanted was to be the object of her gaze.

There were only the two of us on the beach, and being with Sabina was sometimes like being alone. I sat down on the jabbing pebbles, looking out at the sea. Suddenly, I was splashed with water. Sabina ran, giggling and looking over her shoulder at the one who should be chasing her but wasn't. I saw an advantage in restraint and remained sitting. She came back and sat down beside me, stretching out her legs and crossing them at the ankle. A drop of water trickled out from under her dress and down her thigh. She caught me looking and smiled. I smiled back, unembarrassed, but when she leaned in to kiss me, I stared at her chin, unable to risk a look into her eyes. We bumped noses as we kissed. I wanted to tell her something but felt too exhausted, too happy, too vulnerable to say anything.

We walked up the inclining road to the beach house, its lemon-colored walls visible from a distance. We went into the backyard, in the middle of which, on a wooden table, unguarded, lay a pack of cigarettes. I watched the backdoor as Sabina tiptoed to the table, snatched a cigarette, and strolled back with an air of nonchalance, before bursting into laughter. She held the cigarette between index and thumb as we walked down to the beach again, where in a secluded spot near a marked tree, concealed under leaves, a translucent yellow lighter was hidden.

Sabina let out a sudden moan, and I looked for a bird or butterfly, the usual objects of her cooing adoration. But it was a person, ascending the steep road at a quick pace, nothing but a gleam of white to me, that Sabina was pointing at. By the time she began running, I, too, recognized the mysterious man as her father. I approached the embracing couple cautiously.

Sabina's laughter was remote sounding even though it was very near, like the sea.

***

Daniel thought of Sabina in imagistic spurts, mostly as she was the summer he left for America, with a pebble beach in the foreground, the Adriatic in the back, and at the subliminal periphery, a translucent yellow lighter they had hidden beneath rocks and twigs near a marked tree. There's Sabina looking out at the sea, her hands at her side, one leg slightly bent, the strap of her orange dress sliding off her shoulder. There's Sabina dipping her hips to bathe her hands in the blue water, the waves washing over her feet. There's Sabina, arms stretched heavenward, revealing the peach hollow of her smooth armpit, fingers outspread, mouth agape, a mighty yawn, but the corresponding audio is missing and thus a mute roar. Memory is deaf, or clogged with seawater, and he can never hear her yawns, her laughter, her sighs of exasperation.

But he wasn't thinking about her now as he walked across the bustling, tree-lined, and pigeon overrun square on which he had driven miniature cars as a child. He thought he was being perceived as a tourist and it made him feel vulnerable. He had felt it before, this vulnerability, in Trieste, even in Zagreb, but that he should feel it now, here in Mostar, was painful and strange. What imperfection, he wondered, revealed him as an outsider? It couldn't be his wobbly Serbo-Croatian, the clash of accents, because he hadn't said a word. It wasn't what he wore either; his clothes and their clothes were identical. He possessed no foreign odor or aura and must have inherited whatever distinct Bosnian physical characteristics there were. What then?

Daniel himself was uncertain about whether he was a tourist or not, and perhaps this uncertainty was the imperfection. He did not *feel* Bosnian, whatever that meant. Did not *feel* American either. Somewhere in time he had simply ceased being Bosnian without becoming anything else. And why should he not be considered a tourist? Mostar was not really his home, only the place where his father had died.

Crossing the street named after a homegrown poet, Daniel was on Tito's Bridge, going east toward the rugged emerald of some mountain. Once he returned to the States, he began to regret not having paid more attention to his surroundings, not having at his mnemonic disposal readymade images of vivid poignancy when he needed to describe the place of his birth. He regretted not lingering a bit longer on that resurrected bridge, looking down at the southward river, the sinuous, deeply shimmering, almost-turquoise of the cold, clear water, the gray-carved, languid protrusions of stone from which the young, effortless boys leaped. The icy burst of the pearly-green water, the subtly quick current of that beautiful river.

He went down Fejić, the main pedestrian road on the eastern bank, then turned into a small alley that gave out onto a large courtyard called the May 5th Square, according to the daintily written address, his mother's tender hand, on a wrinkled piece of white paper. The half-dilapidated building in which Sabina lived was smaller than Daniel remembered, like everything here, and it didn't have balconies though he distinctly recalled Sabina, afraid of heights and extremely pretty when afraid, clutching the thin black railing as he tried to pry her fingers open. He sat down on a wooden bench in the courtyard, from where he had a view of the building's entrance, not really wanting to see Sabina again, who he had last seen through a train window, waving, and seeming both bored and devastated by his departure. It all came back to him then, sitting there on that brown, wooden, bird-marked bench.

It came to him nearly the way he would later write it down: he and Sabina kneeling on the backseat of the Fiat and looking through the rear window at their fathers, watching them both wave, then become smaller and smaller, and then vanish; the plunging feeling, as he knelt looking out of the rear window, of a remote threat finally revealing its dark significance; Sabina asking him, while both of their parents were outside, arguing with the shaved heads of the border guards, offering passports and papers for their disinterested inspection—she asking him to explain what was going on and he not knowing how to explain, and feeling fear at not knowing, and shame at being afraid. (All I could tell her was that the houses were prettier here, the colors of the flag different from the ones my father had taught me were the colors of my flag.) Sabina running, thin-limbed and blushing, past his mother and up the stairs of the basement, back when the border was but a crouching nightmare in the corner of a dream, back when he and Sabina played adult games in a suddenly adult world, back when Daniel thought that his mother only existed to deny his every satisfaction; a shadowy figure in a lighted doorway taking the shape of his father as he descended the stairs Sabina had just ran up, a smile on his face that Daniel knew was meant for him only, because when his mother turned at the creak of a stair, it disappeared.

The sun, hard and voluptuous, flanked by orange-blue clouds, was setting, and I decided to leave, come back later, at night, if at all. (I never did.) Checking the watch, now on my wrist, I set out toward the Old Bridge.

The street became narrower and narrower, full of people, their faces sinister, mask-like, until they smiled. Small shops, selling worthless knick-knacks, stood on either side. Candles blazed amber in archaic lanterns. Brassy music played out of cafés, laughter and the tinkle of glasses on the terraces. Farther along, more laughter, robust, Slavic-toned laughter, and more music, songs that reminded me of nothing, though I felt they should. Then, the Old Bridge, its white stone as bright as the emerald of the nameless mountain in the background.

As I looked at the bridge, arching over a river whose name I could not recall, I felt what I always felt when I looked upon anything here—a radiant pleasure with a dark tint of pain. The actual Old Bridge, Ottoman built and standing for three centuries, had been destroyed during the war. This was a reproduction, an exact duplicate, built from the old stones, now literally as well as symbolically bridging the two sides of the conflict. Despite the recent reconstruction it was still called the Old Bridge, and, perhaps, for all intents and purposes, it really was. But I knew it was not, nor would it ever be, the bridge over which my father had walked.

The Exile of Muhamed Mehmedbašić

My name is Muhamed Mehmedbašić. I am twenty-eight years old. I am a revolutionary and one of the assassins of Archduke Franz Ferdinand. I am the oldest of the six who took part, according to the Athens newspapers that come here by boat. I was also the sole Muslim, according to the same papers. This does not matter. But that I was the only one to escape does.

After I heard the explosion, I walked toward the train station, leaving my bomb and pistol behind in an alley. I took the first available train to Mostar, unaware of what had happened but believing the archduke was dead. Even so soon after the event, I must admit it did not matter to me anymore. I did not take the train to Mostar because it was home, or because I knew my father was dying there, but because the north and west, the other territories of the Habsburg, were barred to me, and I could not go east to Serbia, whose border with Bosnia, I was certain, must have been already swarming with agents. Home was thus the only place I could return to, though I knew I would not stay there long.

The train left the mountains, and the landscape outside my window softened into plains, where fruit trees—cherry and plum—grew abundant. I knew by the sight of these orchards I was now back in Herzegovina. At the train station in Mostar, on the platform, where men waited to board and pigeons scavenged for food, I did not even think to look over the shoulders of those reading newspapers. It was too early for any news to have reached, anyway. It struck me then that the little money I had in my pockets would not even be enough to buy a newspaper, that, moreover, the only things I possessed were an old pocket watch and the clothes on my back.

It was a cleansing thought.

I entered my boyhood home without any particular feelings, greeted my mother and sisters, and proceeded to my parents' bedroom, where my father lay under a fleece blanket. I sat in an armchair by the side of the bed, as he had done so often at the deathbeds of others. I was not sure if he knew I was there at all. For an hour I sat, watching his chest rise under the dark fleece. We were silent because he could not speak, and I had nothing to say. My mother had closed the door behind me, as if to give our silence privacy. It made me feel like I was in a tomb.

After dinner, I went up to my room on the upper floor and lay on my old bed for a while. Then I went out onto the balcony. From there I could see a bend in the Neretva where the swallows fly over the towers and arch of the Old Bridge. The river was more gray than green in the dusk, and across its narrow width the restaurants and cafés were lit up and filling with men. They did not talk in the excited or hurried tones that bespoke great news, but then it was only in Mostar, among the Muslims of old town, that great news could be discussed without excitement or hurry, in terms of essence, not consequence, here where natural time and sensory time were rarely in agreement. I thought about putting on a jacket and making my way across the river but changed my mind. In one of the restaurants music began to play, a solo male voice backed by an accordion and a tambura. I took a chair out onto the balcony and listened for a long time to the music from the other side. In the distance swallows flecked the dusk sky like scraps of ash.

I dreamed that night of the assassination, as I had thought I would before going to sleep. I awoke the next morning to the news of my father's death, as well as that of the archduke, killed not by the bomb I had heard but by Gavrilo Princip's bullet. I paid my last respects to my father, borrowed some money from my brother-in-law who owned a textile shop in town, and was at the train station by noon. Policemen moved in and out of beams of sunlight that spread over the crowded platform. (When the clouds disappeared altogether, the entire platform was drenched in white light.) They did not search or even question anybody, merely walked about the platform, looking over shoulders and into faces. I stood on the edge of the track and felt, more than once, someone's breath against the back of my neck. I checked my pocket watch; the train was late. Across the tracks, four Habsburg officers and a large German shepherd waited in the shade of a roofed platform. I feared others would be on the train, especially a train headed for Podgorica, but there were none.

I remained in a state of inner paralysis until we crossed the border into Montenegro. It was only when the shock wore off that I began to think about the assassination and my father's death in detail. It occurred to me that I may never see my family again, but soon that thought and the feelings associated with it vanished. I thought about the future but could not envision it. I was going to Podgorica for the same reason I had come to

Mostar, out of the necessity of exile, and my future, like my final destination, would be formed out of that same necessity. Once over the border I instantly felt the freedom of my homelessness.

***

It was perhaps a ten-minute walk from the train station in Podgorica to Stefan Janković's house, where I would stay the night. Stefan was an ethnic Serb and a member of the Black Hand. I knew him from my first exile in Montenegro. We spent the evening drinking homemade walnut brandy in his garden and going over what had happened in Sarajevo. I told him I had stood on the Appel Quay, on the side facing the river, first in the row of assassins that lined the embankment, with a bomb and pistol under my coat. That much was true. I told him, though it was not essential to the story, only to my experience of the event, that I had left behind the cyanide Danilo Ilić had given me that morning because I planned instead to shoot myself right after I threw the bomb. I was afraid of the pain caused by a death from poison, I told him, but I was not afraid to die. I told him that I reached for the bomb as soon as I saw the archduke approach in his car, but just as I was about to take hold of it, a policeman passed close to me, so close, in fact, I felt his warm breath on the back of my neck, and I had to abandon the task.

But there had never been a policeman. This is the first confession I will make here.

The next morning I retold Stefan my story, because he had wanted to hear it again. We were in his garden, which, in the slanting early sunlight, looked much larger than it had the day before. His wife and eldest daughter served us a breakfast that could have fed several men. I noticed how fervently he listened to my every word, how moved he was by our heroism, how intent he seemed on imagining the act that, for me, was already becoming a distant memory. How somber and proud he was when he declared, after I had finished, that war was now inevitable. He was right, surely, but I had not thought about war at all since I had left Sarajevo. I realized then that the event I had experienced only three days ago and had just this morning described for the second time meant more to him than it had ever meant to me. The assassination of the archduke, which for me was but a faint and abstract blow against imperialism, was for Stefan something tangible and significant, something in which notions like brotherhood and fatherland, the very things he spoke of now, were combined without any hint of irony or doubt.

The noon heat drew the scent of the freshly cut grass, which was more pungent than the varied meats and cheeses on the table. A walnut tree gave us shade. Stefan became very serious, even tense, as he ate, and so we ate in silence. After we finished and the table was cleared, he said he had a job for me if I was interested. Gesturing with his hands in a stiff and emphatic way, he told me the story of Nikola Nikolić.

This Nikola Nikolić, a Serb from Bosnia, had been part of a five-man cell, led by Stefan, sent last year to Sarajevo to assassinate Oskar Potiorek, the governor of Bosnia and Herzegovina. More precisely, the men were sent to Ilidža, just outside of Sarajevo, where the Habsburg had built two hotels and a large racecourse, and where Potiorek's country house lay in Mount Igman's shadow. They knew of the governor's habit of taking a horse carriage on Sunday afternoons from his house to the spring of the Bosna River and planned to ambush him en route. They knew the route, for there was only one, a gravel and dirt road running straight from the house to the spring, flanked by large oaks whose fallen leaves choked the path in autumn. Stefan and his men lined themselves up along that road, one at its entrance—where, I remember vividly, gypsy children sold homemade bouquets of fresh lilies and lilacs— and one at the exit, while the other three occupied the kilometer stretch in between. It was these three, with Nikola in the front and Stefan in the middle, who would make the actual attempt on Potiorek's life. The man at the entrance was there to signal the governor's approach, the man at the exit all but a last resort. No explosives were involved in the attack, only pistols, but all five men had served in the Serbian campaigns against the Turks in Macedonia and were capable with their weapons, especially Nikola, a former officer who, Stefan had to admit, was an excellent shot.

The road ran straight enough that each man, equally spaced along the path as they were, could make out the man in front of him and the man behind. At the signal, Nikola immediately started walking toward the entrance and toward the oncoming carriage, and Stefan followed him. People were on the road, and Stefan's men tried to blend into the crowd. Mostly it was bands of children, a few elderly couples, and solitary young men walking in long strides. Nikola too had a long stride, his back narrow and hard and held straight as a rod. The group of people in front of Stefan divided before the carriage like a paper being torn down the middle. They had no choice but to get out of the road completely, onto the mud and grass at the edges, which was what Nikola did without ever taking his eyes off his target. There were four guards, one at each wheel, and two more on the footboard, while behind the carriage trailed more guards on horseback. The roof had been folded back, and Potiorek and his wife, who was expected to be present and spared, if possible, were in full view. The leaves rustled under the wooden wheels, and from his perch the driver shouted in Serbian at some wayward gypsy children. Stefan also remembered the two horses drawing the carriage, how magnificent and bright black they were. Then he saw Nikola take out his pistol and aim it at the governor's heart.

But Nikola hesitated, and he never shot. With his right arm raised and extended, he stood there, frozen in place. Slowly, he turned his head toward Stefan, and there was in Nikola's face an honest anguish that Stefan, when he thought about it later, could not decide was the anguish of a coward or a traitor. The governor's wife screamed, and the magnificent horses came to a sudden standstill. The guard at the rear wheel pounced on Nikola, who did nothing to challenge or resist him, while the guard at the front wheel tracked Nikola's long gaze toward Stefan, who, bewildered by Nikola's action, kept walking hazily in the direction of the carriage. The guard grabbed him by the shoulders, but Stefan, coming to his senses, shook him off and brought him to the ground, then broke through the brambles and oak branches into a wide field and kept running. The column of oaks blocked off the horses and the guards had to chase after him on foot, but Stefan was too fleet and reached the woods at the edge of the field quickly. There, among the looming pine trees, he lost the guards for good.

Not long after, men who knew him began seeing Nikola in the streets of Sarajevo. Stefan had several spies working for the local police, men of high rank who were also Black Hand members. They reported that Nikola had never been brought to the station, meaning he had either escaped during the transfer or was released by the Habsburg authorities since he was one of their agents. It was unclear to me, since it was unclear to Stefan, if Nikola was indeed a double agent or if he had acted out of cowardice. Stefan did know that Nikola eventually fled to Greece, most likely through Macedonia, ending up in Athens. Through a source in Athens, a man I would meet later, Stefan found out that Nikola was now on Serifos, an island in the western Cyclades.

I agreed to the task without speaking a word; we merely clinked our glasses of brandy. Nikola's betrayal, whatever had inspired it, did not matter to me. What did matter was the need to seek shelter as far from Sarajevo as possible, and nothing at that moment seemed farther away than this oblique island in the Aegean. I had never even heard of the place. A sudden image of the island flared up in my mind but just as soon faded out.

***

Stefan supplied me with a forged passport that he said would get me safely to Greece. But first we had to get across the border to Serbia. For this purpose I was joined by Filip, a smuggler who knew the best spot to cross the border. Stefan introduced me by my given name, and I at once noticed Filip's eyes narrow contemptuously. We shook hands. In the cart I rode up front with him, but we did not speak. This did not bother me, for the idle joy that belongs only to passengers is merely heightened by the driver's silence.

We easily slipped by the frontier guards on Montenegro's border with Serbia and were now in Kosovo, which Filip referred to, reverently, as Old Serbia. We had stopped near a small gray church on a hill to rest the horses and drink from the well in the courtyard. It was then, after he had taken a sip of the water and exhaled that he said, "Ah, Old Serbia," as though he had taken a long sip of the land itself. He had spoken to no one in particular when he said it, and yet, he had spoken to everything and everyone present at that moment—to me, to the valley below us, to the surrounding pinewood, to the well and the wild roses that had sprung up around it, to the gray hill and the gray church perched atop it like a falcon atop a crag. The water from the well was cold and fresh, like a cucumber.

We rode along the edge of the valley, half of which lay in the bluest shade, between hills forested with pines. By nightfall we reached the train station in Peč, and there we parted with a handshake. I took the night train to Priština, sleeping fitfully, and arrived in the city by morning. The train station in Priština was lively with the disorder of mobilization, soldiers having either just arrived from the south or traveling northward toward the capital. Their faces shone with energy and anticipation as they laughed and joked out on the platform, wedged comfortably, it seemed to me, between the expectations of a proud past and the promise of a glorious future, both of which were an illusion.

I had boarded my train to Ohrid without difficulty and was watching the soldiers from the window when the train jolted forward. Soon I was passing fields of long grass and rosebushes, and stone crosses hung with wreaths of poppies. I remembered the gray church on the hill. I thought of the mosque in Mostar, its high dome and the light coming through the high windows, and the curving and twining lines of the Arabic calligraphy, and me in my bare feet, the cold of the flat stones against my

soles, with my father close beside. How, on our knees, flank to
flank, we bowed like slaves.

The train was now passing a village, its ramshackle houses
and decaying farmland, gray, yellow, and green fields, flocks of
sheep—white sheep, black sheep—and peasants in their old and
dirty clothes, enlivened by embroidery, their backs stooped and
mouths open. I saw barefoot children run after the train at a
distance, cheerful, probably illiterate. I could tell these people
were Christian, though poverty made no distinction, here or
anywhere, between one creed and another. What did they have
to do with Old Serbia? A violent feeling rose inside me, but I
repressed it, or it was overcome by the lethargy of the train ride.

***

I arrived in Ohrid in the early evening, checked into a hotel,
and fell asleep before the sun set over the lake that gave this
town its name. I awoke fully rested, the lone window open,
the cool air blowing off the lake and into my room. I had my
coffee in the courtyard of a café that stood near the bakery in
which I'd had breakfast. The courtyard was oblong and sun-
filled. From where I sat, I had a good view of the hilltop ruins
of a Roman fortress built on an Illyrian foundation. Four men
sat at a nearby table, and except for us and an old waiter who
ran about or stood leaning against the door to the café, the
courtyard was empty. There had been only three men when I
sat down, the fourth arriving soon after. It was at him that the
conversation was directed; he seemed to have just returned from
what must have been a long absence and was now being brought
up to date by his friends. All four men spoke in Serbian, not
Macedonian, and their Serbian lacked the peculiar accent with

which native Macedonians spoke. They were a very loud and boastful group of young men, though all the stories they told, from what I could gather, were mostly mundane reminiscences, until one of them began telling the others of a duel.

The name of the storyteller was Nikola too, and he was perhaps the youngest of the four; twenty, I would say, by the look of him. He wore spectacles, distinguishing him from the other three by giving his face a more somber look. Though not a natural storyteller, he spoke with a nervous excitement that implied he was telling the others all he knew. What he told them was how one winter night he got a visit from Valon, who asked if he would act as a second to a fellow Serb that Valon was going to fight a duel against in the morning. All but the fourth man, the one who had returned after a long absence, knew of Valon, a drunkard and also an Albanian, who was a regular at the tavern the men patronized. A young, morose, eccentric man, a character, if not a fiction, Valon had once broken a glass over some accordionist's head during a disagreement. Still, the fourth man could not remember Valon, nor that particular incident. Nikola moved on, telling them—though he was really only speaking to the fourth man, for perhaps the other two had heard the story before—that after he agreed to the task, which he did without much thought, Valon gave him the time and place. They were to meet at dawn, at a remote cove famous as a meeting place for secret lovers. All four of the men knew of this cove, its tantalizing isolation, its dreamy luridness. They seemed to me, despite their insinuations, to be more acquainted with the myth of such a place than its reality.

Nikola arrived early at this cove, which I imagine was shaped like a crescent moon, half-surrounded and hidden by limestone cliffs and boulders except for a narrow, sloping entrance, though this description may be more true of the coves of this island than those found in Ohrid. Nikola described the sky that morning as violet and pale green, the lake a pale, glassy orange. The sun was mottled like an iguana, he said. Someone urged him to get to the good part already. He had arrived earlier than the time he had been given and walked along the curving stretch of sand beach, waiting for the others. As he approached one end of the cove, the darkness now fully lifted, he noticed a man sitting among the bulky, charred-looking rocks near the water. As though aware that Nikola had noticed him, the man stood up and began walking in his direction. Nikola was certain that this man had been watching him all along. They shook hands, laughed at how fitting it was, one Nikola as a second to the other. Then, in a sober tone, Nikola, the duelist, thanked Nikola, the second, for coming. They were quiet for what Nikola said seemed to him a long time, both of them watching a gull stranded on a piece of driftwood out on the lake.

There was much Nikola wanted to ask, but he remained silent, because silence seemed at that moment to be the correct manner in which the business of a second was to be conducted, especially a second to a man such as the one who now, silently and inexplicably, stood beside Nikola on this remote beach. When minutes later Valon arrived with his second, a cousin of his, Nikola already felt he had, by his mere silence, earned the other Nikola's complete and utter trust, and that they therefore shared a deep understanding that went beyond any knowledge acquired through words, even though Nikola was well aware he knew nothing of his enigmatic namesake, least of all why he was standing beside him now on this remote beach. He moved toward Valon and his second while the other Nikola, either unaware of Valon's presence or pretending to be, kept looking across the lake, past the gull and the driftwood, past a small island in the distance, all the way toward the Albanian coast. Valon's gaze over the shoulder of one Nikola toward the other was quietly but openly hostile. Valon was well-dressed, but in a gaunt, untidy way. Dark, ignorant, volatile, needy, he stood, his shoulders stooped, in stark contrast to Nikola, the duelist, who turned toward him now, with only curiosity and intelligence in his eyes, offering Valon his hand. They held each other's gaze during the handshake and the brief talk that followed—a blank, stony exchange of words. Valon hid his evident panic behind a fierce stare, while the other Nikola showed neither courage nor fear in his face, hiding only his amusement.

Valon's second presented the pistols to both Nikolas for inspection. The number of steps was randomly agreed upon as twelve. The duelists stood back to back and then began to walk toward their respective seconds, who had marked the spots where they should turn. Nikola watched the other Nikola come closer, watched the muted dance of his long, slow strides. His expression unreadable, he, the duelist Nikola, held the pistol in his right hand like it was but a toy. The cove was silent except for the wind, which was sometimes wild laughter, sometimes dark fury, and the incessant splash of the waves. The rocks were brass-colored in the rising sun, the sand still cold from the night. Nikola swallowed to keep his voice from shaking as he wished the other Nikola good luck. He nodded solemnly, and Nikola found the gesture intelligent. More than intelligent, wise. Nikola, the duelist, turned to face Valon, his spine straight, almost rigidly so. With an aristocratic air to his inscrutability, he looked, Nikola said, as noble as a Byzantine.

It occurred to Nikola that despite their obvious differences, there existed, for a moment at least, an abstract harmony between the duelists as they faced each other across a distance of twelve steps, their eyes staring at a common center—the harmony of a man with his image in the mirror. Valon raised his pistol, and Nikola wondered, standing to the side of the other Nikola, a few steps away, how sensitive his body must have been now to everything outside of his body—the breeze, the spray, the bullet. There was a crack, then a bang. Nikola's heart emptied, then refilled. Valon had aimed for the head, there was no doubt, but had missed over the shoulder.

The other Nikola's eyes had closed, and now they blinked open again. He had reacted, in Nikola's opinion, as any dignified man would when so suddenly alerted to his own mortality. Now it was his turn and Nikola, the duelist, raised his pistol, his arm firm, his throat clenched, his mouth tight as a fist. But his pistol, Nikola noticed, was pointed just above Valon, up toward the large, insistent mountains—which intrude themselves on our awareness, Nikola said—and that was where he sent his shot. He might as well have shot straight into the air, Nikola said. But pity clothed in honor was preferable to naked pity. Nikola the duelist shouted to ask Valon if he was satisfied; Valon opened his mouth but could only nod. The duel was over. Nikola walked over to Valon, shook his hand, shook the hand of his second, disposed of the weapon, turned back toward Nikola the second, shook his hand as well, and then disappeared up the slope.

I could not see what kind of impression the story had made on the fourth man, for he sat with his back to me. Then I suddenly realized that the tale was told not for his benefit but mine. I looked at Nikola, and indeed he was looking back at me, though only briefly, and seemingly without meaning.

I left the café convinced that the Nikola of the story was the Nikola I was sent to find. I took a narrow cobblestone street to the water, passing the central square, which was crowded and noisy because of the market there. It was mostly people from nearby villages selling poultry and vegetables and garlic and spices, or local women, all of them either very old or very young, selling jewelry and fabrics. One of the older women who sold wool had a face reminiscent of my mother's. Her black stockings hung loose around her calves. I thought of my mother, how damp and bright her eyes had become at my goodbye. And I thought of the weeping that came after I was gone. I went back into the alley and continued down toward the water. The Serbian flag, with its double-headed eagle, hung above the door of a building. I passed under it. The Albanian flag too, I recalled, bore the emblem of a double-headed eagle. I thought of the Macedonian flag but could not visualize it. Reaching the promenade, I went east, away from the mountains and toward the mountains.

I inquired after the whereabouts of the Muslim quarter because that was where I was headed, though another part of me wanted to walk down the promenade until it came to an end, then walk on the sand to the water, then at the edge of the water either turn left or right with the knowledge that there was nothing to gain or lose whichever way I turned. The horizon began to slowly pale, the reds and golds and dark blues all fading. A grief came over me that was not based on any rational feeling of unhappiness, for I was not unhappy.

I took the street I was told and made my way uphill, away from the promenade. And then it came, the somber absurdity of the call to prayer. The mosque in Ohrid was too small, the men gathered to worship spilling out into the courtyard, every part covered, except for where a fountain stood. The men kneeled down and bowed toward the earth while I watched them from the gate. When it was over, I asked the men coming through the gate if they knew if Valon was here or where he lived. Most of the Muslims in Ohrid, if not all, were Albanians, and Valon was a popular name among them, so I described him by way of the incident with the accordionist. A young man walked me to his own house, which he said faced the back of Valon's. I asked him why Valon had not gone to the service, and he said that Valon had not been in a while. Then he said they were only neighbors, and he did not know Valon well.

A short fence which I easily climbed divided the young man's yard from Valon's. Manure stood piled against the stone wall of what looked like a pigpen but certainly had no pigs in it. A goat tied to an ash tree came near me, stretching its chain. I went around to the front, where there was a vegetable garden not unlike the vegetable garden at the front of our house. I knocked on the door and was received by a woman heavily veiled— Valon's mother. The hallway over her shoulder separated into a staircase on the left and a narrow passage on the right. She guided me down the narrow passage, then moved against the wall to let me pass, tucking her shoulders in. Her eyes, the only part of her that was visible, looked away from mine.

We talked, Valon and I, sitting on the floor. His room was bare in a poignant way, and it smelled of stale dust. Like a room in a monastery, I thought. Books stood in high stacks against the far wall. A prayer rug lay unrolled beneath the only window. On a blue plate at his side were three figs and a piece of brown bread. I had interrupted his supper, he said, as he sat cross-legged. He spoke in a soft voice, in a pronounced, strange,

tortured Serbian. I apologized for intruding on him like this
and introduced myself not by my given name or the name on
my forged passport, David Danon, but as Kemal Karabegović,
a name I had used before. I told Valon I was looking for a man
named Nikola Nikolić, a man he knew.

"Who told you I know him?" he asked.

"I cannot say," I said.

"Why are you looking for him?"

"I cannot say that either."

"It does not matter," he said, almost smugly. "I can guess
both answers."

I wanted to ask him about the duel but asked instead why he
had not been at the mosque today. He did not seem surprised by
the question and said he could not stand the imam's hypocrisy
anymore, which I thought both an exact and vague answer. He
said that religion betrays us with its myriad consolations and
that he no longer wished to be betrayed or consoled.

"But you still pray," I said, eyeing the prayer rug.

"I still believe in God, and prayer is the only way I know to
communicate with Him. But I pray in private, which is the only
true way. Before, when I went to the mosque, I did not believe
in God. It is only now that He's become real to me."

"You don't drink anymore either?"

"I do not, no."

"Did all these changes occur after the duel?" I asked.

"No," he said. "The duel made the changes only more urgent."

"Was it a blood feud?"

He grinned cryptically. "Yes, but only in the sense that all
conflicts between men are blood feuds."

"Why did you challenge him?"

"Because he dishonored my sister by wanting to marry her."
He thought about it for a while, then he said, without emphasis,
"Because he dishonored me by asking for her hand."

"You fought to reclaim her honor, and yours?"

"My family's honor, yes. They have taken everything from
us, but they will never take our honor."

"The Serbs?"

"Who else but those pig farmers? Where are you from?"

"Sarajevo," I said. "I was born in Mostar."

"Yes, I thought you were from Bosnia. You must know then
what I'm talking about. Bosnia will go the way of Macedonia,
and you will suffer the way we suffer."

He spoke of the first war, in which he did not fight for either
side, Serbian or Turkish, because he had believed both to be
foreign powers, equal in their oppression. He spoke of the
second war, where again and for the same reasons he did not
choose sides, Serbian or Bulgarian. He spoke bitterly of life
now, under Serbian rule. He spoke of Serbs not with a hatred
of Serbs, but with a hatred of the Serbs' hatred for all those who
are themselves not Serbs. He spoke fearfully and mockingly
of a greater Serbia. Wherever there are Serbs, there will be
only Serbs, he said, with fear, with mocking. He spoke of the
threat the assassination in Sarajevo posed to all non-Serbs and
described the assassins, whoever they were, as false prophets.

"Their freedom is our tyranny," he said, pointedly.

"You and I, we are not the same."

"Is your God not Allah?"

I was silent.

Valon began to talk of God, and I had a strange absence of
feeling toward his words. Sensing, perhaps, that the thread with

which he had tried to connect us was too short for use on my end, he stopped talking of Allah.

"No, we are not the same," he said. "You are Bosnian and I'm Albanian. But we are the same in the sense that neither of us is a Serb." He waited for me to respond, but I only nodded. "We are the same in the sense that their freedom is our tyranny."

"Do you know where Nikola is now?"

"I don't care where he is."

"Does your sister know?"

"She also doesn't care."

Of the duel, when I asked him, he said only that he had survived.

"That is all?" I asked.

"That is everything," he said.

I got up to leave, but he did not get up with me. We did not shake hands.

In the hallway I saw his sister coming down the stairs. Unveiled, she quickly turned away from me and pressed her face against the wall. A severe gesture, surprising and unforgettable. I knew she would stay like that until I left, like a woman turned to stone. I pitied her immensely. I remembered my own sisters, how protective and shy I was of them, more so the older we got. They always spoke to me with great freedom but also from a great distance.

As I walked back to the hotel, I looked for the moon, but there was none. The promenade was deserted, the mountains silhouettes. I paid my bill and took the last train out. Another hotel, another train, another life. It began to rain on the way to the station, a hard rain, like before a storm, though the storm never came, or perhaps the train kept us ahead of it. I was sure it was the first rain since the night before the assassination. It was a long, sleepless train ride into Greece, but the rain is all I remember.

***

Along with the forged passport and some money, Stefan gave me a letter of introduction to Branislav Ivanović, the man I was to see in Athens and from whom I was to get information about Nikola. I followed a crudely drawn map, also given to me by Stefan, crossing a couple of large squares in the naked sun to the man's house in the Plaka, a neighborhood of narrow and tightly intertwining streets sloping uphill toward the Parthenon. The shops and cafés, which made the narrow streets even narrower and more deeply shaded, were reminiscent of Sarajevo. I knocked on the door of his house several times before a thickset man of middle age answered. He looked as though he had just been woken. I asked if he was Branislav Ivanović, and he grumbled yes. I introduced myself by my given name, certain that it was the name used in the letter, which I handed to him. He skimmed it, distracted by something behind him, for he kept looking over his shoulder as he read. I could hear footsteps and the creak of stairs. The door was open a quarter and he filled that quarter of space with his mass. He threw the letter to the side, apparently satisfied by its contents, and told me to meet him in an hour in a café off the Monastiraki Square. The door closed, and I saw myself vaguely reflected in the dark wood.

At the Monastiraki Square I sat in the heavy shade of the mosque that was no longer a mosque, eating a lamb gyro from a vendor. Taking my time, I ate and watched the people go by: Greeks with their brown arms and necks; Turks too, just as there are still Greeks in Istanbul; gypsies, whose faces were the deepest shade of brown; and also a few Westerners, recognizable by their pale arms and sunburned faces. A young girl stood in the middle of the square, selling strawberries out of a basket, her legs naked and brown. I waited until the appointed time, checking my pocket watch, wanting him to arrive before me.

The café was on the side of a busy thoroughfare. The glare in my eyes made it impossible to look down any significant length of the street. It made me focus on what was close at hand. He was there when I arrived, sitting in the half shade under the edge of the awning, wearing a faded white suit, almost gray now, and a straw hat with a silk band, which he wore so far back on his head it looked like a halo. The café was full of voices and smoke. I went up to him, expecting him to be angry at being kept waiting, but he was surprisingly jovial.

"Where's your hat?" he asked, standing up to shake my hand. "You need a hat here."

"Hats are a nuisance," I said. "An absurdity of the West."

"Be that as it may, you need a hat here. And clothing light in color."

I asked him how he had found Nikola, and he told me he came across him at a tavern near the train station in Omonoia Square. The tavern was called Belgrade, after the owner's birthplace.

"It is where all the Serb émigrés in Athens congregrate," Branislav Ivanović said. Then he said, "Athens is like a dream, and in a dream one meets all kinds of people. Nikola walked into the tavern that night as unexpectedly and in the same strange manner people from one's past walk into one's dream. I knew right away it was him. That face, I would recognize it anywhere. A man can change his name, but not his face, or his fate."

He lit a cigarette and leaned back in his chair. "I had received letters from Stefan, I knew all that had happened, and all that I knew came rushing back to me at the sight of that face. I should have finished it then and there, but Greece is a democracy, a democracy in the Western style, moreover, which means murder, however justified, is still a punishable offence. He surveyed the room in a confident manner, but as soon as he saw me looking at him, his confidence was gone. Needless to say, he didn't hang around too long. He said a few things to the bartender and left."

I asked Ivanović how he knew Nikola, and he only said that he knew him from the war, without going into any more detail. Then I asked him what had happened next. He talked to the bartender himself and found out that Nikola had been coming in for days, usually in the morning, that he sat by himself at the bar, quiet, morose, nursing his drink, listening to the talk of others. The bartender did not know where he was staying, where he was going, or where he had been, knew nothing, in fact, but his name, Konstantin Levin. Then, suddenly, the bartender thought of something else, how Konstantin had once asked him about Serifos, wanting to know what the island was like and if the bartender knew anyone who had been there. But the bartender knew nothing of the island and nobody who had gone to Serifos or come back from it.

"The only reason you think Nikola is on Serifos is because he mentioned the island once to a bartender?"

"That piece of information is all we have. But I can tell you that he is no longer here in Athens. If you had seen his face when he saw me, you would be as certain as I am that he left the very next morning. And if he had come this far south, he was certainly not going back north again. My gut tells me he is on one of those islands, and Serifos is as good a bet as any."

"This is a fool's errand," I said.

"What does it matter to you?" he asked, leaning toward me, one elbow on the table.

I did not know what to say, and he knew I did not. Suddenly I wondered what Stefan had written in that letter of introduction and regretted not reading it before handing it to him.

"It matters to Stefan," I said, without conviction, and Ivanović let out a short laugh.

"Stefan is an old and dear friend of mine, a good man, a real patriot, but he is too trustful. I told him not to get involved with a Jew."

"Nikola is Jewish? How do you know that?"

"My gut, Muhamed. Something about his manner, his face, that nose, that name, Konstantin Levin, which I think is his given name, and not the least his traitorous act. He is certainly now as homeless as a Jew. I do not mind them all, some make for great revolutionaries, but most are, due to their inherent nature, poor nationalists."

"Konstantin Levin is a character out of a Russian book," I said.

"Nevertheless. The revolution is over, and we don't need their kind to poison our efforts to build a common Slav state. The next war will be a war of independence and our motivation must shift accordingly. It is a nationalist cause we are fighting for now. The Habsburg hate and pity us but we will rid ourselves of their pity even if doing so strengthens their hate for us. For they will always hate us, but now the burden of their hate will find no relief in pity. They wanted from us what they themselves would never accept, complete and total submission. After Sarajevo they want it more than ever. Because we dared to defend ourselves, they call us terrorists. But we were merely resisting occupation, is that not right? We will resist it until the end of time."

As he spoke I felt a powerful ambivalence toward his words, like when Valon had spoken of Allah. It was as though I had not a single binding root left in my body.

"No one wants war," he went on, gesturing with his cigarette, "but it is a necessity. It draws you as much as it repels you, but it will come. When it does we must fight it together, all the southern Slavs as one, be they Orthodox or Catholic, or Muslim. War is preferable to slavery. I love freedom, Muhamed, and it is freedom that gives me the courage to fight. Jews, they find their freedom only in wandering and treachery. They will not fight with us Slavs."

"And when there is a common Slav state, what then?"

"Then we shall be happy. Then exiles like you and I shall finally return home."

The sunlight was oblique and blinding; on the street it hardened the edges around things. Ivanović lit another cigarette. I pondered the word *home*. It filled me with immense doubt.

"When the Habsburg are gone, who will fill the vacuum of power they leave behind?"

"The Serbs, naturally. We must be realistic here, my friend. Diplomacy is a matter of power, and Serbia is the most powerful country in our region, and it is up to Serbia to establish and maintain a land for all the Slavs of southern Europe. Let me assure you, what is in the best interest of Serbia is also in the best interest of Bosnia. We will be sensitive to the hurt of others, for we are more sensitive to hurt than any others, for no other people have suffered as much hurt as us. Our situation is indeed exceptional."

"Whose situation? The Slavs' or the Serbs'?"

His voice rose under the smoke. "Both," he said. "But the Serbs' situation is the most exceptional of all. As a state we must work toward universal moral principles, of course. But in certain aspects Serbia must embrace an imperial role: the Albanian question, for example. There must be rules, of course. We are not anarchists! But there needs to be one country that creates the rules, and enforces those rules, and that, at certain times, must not be bound by those rules."

"I see." I readied myself to leave. "I will take the next ferry to Serifos and will write to Stefan when it is all done."

"God be with you, Muhamed," he said. The sun was in his eyes now and he adjusted his hat. I knew he would sit there readjusting his hat to the movement of the sun until the sun set, go to the tavern to speak of revolution and war, and then take home a prostitute who would stay until the morning, when he would return back to this café.

I took a tram to Piraeus. The harbor was large, the largest I had ever seen. The air smelled overwhelmingly of fish. While waiting for the ferry, I bought a hat. Then the ferry came. From the back of the boat, I watched the land recede into a sliver of coastline, until that too vanished. I went to the front where there were some chairs. The sun was beating down, and there were not many people out. The sea and sun smoothed the distance between here and there, near and far. The rocking of the boat dulled my muscles. I tipped the hat over my forehead and fell asleep, slumped in a chair. I dreamed of my father. When I awoke, I could see the island, a barren rock, hills tapering and rising. I leaned over the railing, watching the island come closer, noticing the houses, white and spare. Here I was, and here I still am, on this island, neither out of chance nor design, it seems. The journey had been as much a moving away as a moving toward, but from what and toward what, I am not sure anymore. I was only certain of the urgency to keep moving. I no longer feel this urgency as strongly, not now, not yet. The anchor dropped. I had arrived. The ferry was still. The water settled, calm like stone.

***

Only a few people exited the ferry, and soon it was on its way to more popular islands in the Aegean. Later I found out that the ferries only stopped one day a week at the port of Serifos, and I just happened to pick that day. A Thursday, I think. Perhaps I had been lucky. Perhaps, fated. I checked into the only hotel here, Hotel Perseus, named after the first exile to this island, thinking Nikola must have stayed in this hotel too, if he had ever been here at all. When I woke up the next morning, I had forgotten where I was. Once I recovered my senses, a different kind of disorientation took over, the kind you feel on your first walk through a strange town or city, the kind you only appreciate after you know the place and its wonders are lost. I have loved that feeling always and felt it everywhere. I often wish I could have that feeling with me all the time, even after the familiarity has set in, but at that moment it is irrecoverable, except in memory, where the place of those earliest days, the place I remember, is no longer the place I am in.

Out in the courtyard of the hotel, facing the water, I knew that turning right would take me toward the pier, so I went left on the paved street that stretched along the beach and curved uphill. It was not paved for long, becoming a dirt road, red dust rising. House after house, whitewashed, with blue shutters; little goats in their small pastures of short, sun-paled grass. After a while I began to walk on the sand, hearing the soft rattle beneath and behind each step. The sound of sand on sand made me think there was another traveler on my heels, aping my gait. But I was the only person on the beach that morning. The sand was gray and dimpled, browner and more thickly packed near the water, with a few small red or blue boats dotting the shore. I retook the path, which curved broadly uphill, then steadied, and then bent and dipped toward a small bay. I headed toward the bay almost at a run, scattering sand onto fallen tree bark. It sounded like sugar being sifted onto wood. The sand was finer at this beach, and whiter.

A church stood above the shore, on a ledge in the cliffside, overlooking the bay. It stood on a cliff like the church in Kosovo had stood on a hill, fantastical, alone. It was not gray like a falcon but white like a seagull. Stairs led up to it, but its door was locked. The water below was a very bright blue in the sun, a much darker blue beneath the ragged shadow of the cliff.

This is my final confession, for since I have come to this monastery, I have been without sin. The hotel owner's daughter, who worked numerous jobs within the hotel, was on the brink of her sexual vitality, a borderline that had engaged my imagination for many years now. On the first morning, at breakfast in the courtyard, she came up to my table and asked, in Serbian, if I was Serbian. I tried to explain what I was, but she did not understand, either because she did not understand the concept of a Bosnian (I did not say I was Muslim) or because her

Serbian was not strong enough. Yes, I said finally, I'm Serbian.
She had a round, pretty face. She was seventeen. I asked how
she knew Serbian, and she said her mother, who was dead, had
been Serbian on her father's side. I could sense by the change in
her eyes, by the new inflection her voice took on as she began to
speak of other things, that she had lied to me. Certainly about
her mother being any part Serbian, perhaps about her mother
being dead too. She wore no stockings; the blond fuzz of her
brown legs shone in the sunlight. I confess that as I swam in the
waters under the church, I thought of her legs and the young
fullness of her breasts.

Her name was, and still is, Peatrice. I have not seen her since
I've come to live in this monastery.

That night, after my walk and a nap, I had dinner in the
courtyard. I may have been the only guest of the hotel in that
courtyard, the rest locals who had come in to eat or for a drink.
There were two men, one young, one old—father and son, I found
out later—with bouzoukis, and they played late into the night.
The old man sang. Peatrice was waitressing, but sometimes she
stopped her work and started to dance, the tray in her hand like
a tambourine. She took small, halting steps in rhythm with the
music, stomping her foot to the beat. Though only seventeen, the
movement of her hips was intensely feminine. I could not tell any
of the songs apart; they were all beautiful, faintly somber, fusing
into one another. During one of her dances, with her father in the
courtyard watching her from a table, I went inside and flipped
through the guestbook in the dim light of the match I had struck.
Most were Greek, a few English, a few German, one French, then,
almost three months to the day before my own arrival, a man
named Vladimir Lensky.

I came late to breakfast the next morning and found her clearing a table in the courtyard, bent over, humming to herself. I touched her gently and her shoulders jerked. As she served me, her gaze was both searching and shy, fearful and indirect, but not very subtle. I asked her about Vladimir Lensky, a friend of mine who had stayed here before. Did she remember him at all? She thought about it for a moment, the name, the man, then shook her head, no. When she reached for my empty cup of coffee I felt a terrible urge to grab her by the wrist and ask her again. Instead, I went for a long walk and avoided Peatrice for the rest of the day.

The next morning she was not there to serve my breakfast. Her brother, a child of thirteen, was the waiter for the day, a Sunday. She came back in the afternoon. I cornered her in the upstairs hallway as she delivered towels to the rooms. I asked where she had been. She told me she had gone to the Hora, the old town on top of the hill, for supplies. She pretended she could not understand my other question, dipping her shoulders beneath my outstretched arm.

The next day, a Monday, she was at the hotel the entire time. On Tuesday she did not go anywhere either. Wednesday as well. We spoke less and less, but there was still a vivid sense of back and forth between us: she was gravely watchful of my every movement, and I of hers.

On Thursday, a week after I landed on this island, I went up to the Hora, a narrow, bare, sun-beaten and steep, steep path. I realized at once that if I had tried to follow her, as I had initially planned, there would have been no cover for me at all. She would only have needed to turn her head to see me. No place to hide for safety, I thought, slowly making my way up. No place to hide in ambush either.

When I reached the top, the path opened onto a small square. I sat in the only café there, pretending to read a newspaper and checking my pocket-watch. Something told me she would not be able to wait longer than three days to visit him again. After a half hour, she came carrying a basket. She did not turn left toward all the houses layered atop of each other and crowding the hill, but went right, past a windmill and out of the old town, back into the island wild. I followed her, but only as far as the windmill, behind which I hid and watched her. She rose and dipped, casting a long shadow against the round rocks, steady and quick, her back straight with purpose. Slowly, she disappeared into the distance, the brown land, the white light. Up on another hill, there stood a building, indistinct in the brightness. I knew it was this building she was walking toward for there was no other kind of shelter as far as the eye could see.

I did nothing for the next few days, waiting for a strong feeling to arise from the depths of my paralysis. I stayed in bed past noon, then walked the island, and both felt to me the same, both a kind of waiting. I waited so long to act I lost count of the days. I walked the backstreets, past small farms and stables, feeding the donkeys and mules that thrust their heads over the fence. I walked the hills, tipping my hat to the same old shepherd whose sheep chocked the trail. He raised his gnarled stick, a gnarled figure himself, dark from the sun and robed like a monk. Only women and children and old men were in the street during the week; most of the men my age worked the mines on another part of the island. They did not come home at night. Geese appeared on the path that ran along the beach, snapping at each other, fighting in the rising dust.

Gulls skimmed the water with their breasts, shells hanging from their beaks. I lay on the beach under the church, which had regained its ordinariness. I walked the farthest reaches of the island, as far as my legs could take me. I found desolote coves in whose waters I swam until evening. At night the music would start up in the courtyard, and I would lie on the bed in my room, listening. I noticed that Peatrice had not left the hotel since the day I had seen her on the Hora. Still I waited. I watched her, but she no longer watched me. I was running low on money and would soon be unable to pay for the room. Still I waited.

Then one morning I awoke knowing I would go to visit the monastery.

By noon I was on the Hora, making my way past the windmill and into the brown and gray landscape: rocks and earth and scrub, but also green grass and long, reedlike flowers that bent in the wind. From the top of the monastery, one could already see me coming, though I was not even halfway there. Gray rocks and gray scrub and brown earth, but also a narrow stream by which I rested, soaking my handkerchief in the cold water and draping it over my forehead. The pebbles looked rounder and glossier at the bottom of the stream than in my palm. Past the stream it was a steep climb to the monastery. I tried to make out the writing arched over the large wooden door, but my Greek was meager. I understood each letter, written in black paint, understood each word, but their combination was an abstraction. The door was open, so I entered the monastery. Cavernous walls curved over a white church in the light-filled courtyard. Sunlight and stillness, except for a rustling from above. Up the stairs a honeycomb of rooms rose above the terrace, from where the rustling was coming. The colored doors of the rooms—blue, violet, pink— were so small that even a man of average size would have to bow to go through them. I imagined the interior of the rooms, small, bare, dark prison cells, though one could enter and exit at will.

I followed the rustling sound out onto the terrace where four leather-bound books were left open to dry on the parapet, their pages turning in the wind.

On the left-hand side of each page was writing in black ink, and on the right-hand side were watercolor paintings. Wetness still showed at the side and bottom of each page, the thin paper translucent as the wind lifted and turned it toward the sunlight. The rustling was the only sound in the monastery, amplifying the silence. Below the parapet the land arched and vaulted, dipped into valleys and rose into hills, then sloped toward the beaches and gave way to the sea.

I felt the monk's presence before he spoke.

"I have read these books so often that I have come to feel that I have written them," he said in my language. His head was shaved, his beard long. He wore a blue robe that stopped just short of his sandaled feet, a broad red band around his waist.

"Do you still believe every word?"

He bowed over one of the books. "I admit some of it does not ring true to me anymore."

"How do you speak my language so well?"

"I have studied in Belgrade. And fought with a Serb battalion in Kosovo. I have had some recent practice as well." He paused, either thinking about what he had said or what he was going to say next. "I was told of your coming by the one you seek."

"Where is he?"

"Nikola is gone."

For some reason his name, spoken out loud, startled me. "What was he doing here," I asked, "in the monastery?"

"He labored lightly. Cleaned the rooms, swept the floors, the terrace, watered the plants, took care of the books. He had

put these out to dry; it was the last thing he did. He tended
the chickens as well; we have a chicken coop on the other side.
When we had foreign visitors, he showed them around. We do
get some tourists here. The more barren the land, the more holy,
they think. But nothing on God's earth is barren, not even the
deserts."

I looked at the monk again in his simple robe and sandals.
"Why did he come here?"

"That I don't know. When I asked him, he told me it was
need and chance, neither of which he entirely understood, that
had brought him here, to this place he did not know. He was
talking about the monastery, but he could as well have been
talking about all of Serifos, or any place he had been, including
the place he was from. What is your name?"

"Muhamed."

"Why do you suppose he was here, Muhamed? Why are you
really here?"

I shrugged.

"Men like Nikola, and perhaps you too are that kind of man,
they want to be brave and innocent, they want to be both at
once, which is impossible. And you cannot return to innocence
after you have been brave. Nikola had come here, I suppose, to
do just that, return to innocence. But only Christ could do that.
Only Christ could be brave and innocent at once."

"Why did he leave?"

"When he came here he was on the verge of disintegration,
physically, mentally, spiritually. Ideas by which he had lived
had shown their emptiness to him, lost their authority, became
only words. One has to choose between obedience and doubt,
Muhamed. Nikola came here to seek redemption, but even here

he found it compromised. His eyes were sober and his mouth bitter when he came, and they remained that way. Again, he was given a choice between obedience and doubt, and again he chose doubt. An exile by nature, Nikola always chose doubt."

"What do you mean?"

He looked straight into my eyes as he spoke. "Man depends on certainty," he said, "but the world he inhabits cannot be reduced to a man's certainty. Doubt blurs borders that certainty erects. A man in doubt is therefore a man in perpetual exile. Nikola was such a man. A stranger to his land, to his time, a stranger to his own history and therefore to his own reality. He was exiled from the revolutionary politics he once practiced, exiled from the nationalism of those around him, exiled too from religion. All he knew of religion was its subtle cynicism, its dark corners in which there was no room for transcendence. Once, right after the assassination of the archduke, in fact, he told me he was beyond salvation. Like a Jew, I thought. He may well have been one, a Jew, for he only told me he was an atheist. But the atheism of men like Nikola was of no good. It could not free him of his sense of guilt, only of the hope of absolution."

"This island, then, was to be the place of his final exile?"

"By leaving the mainland behind, he convinced himself he was leaving history behind. Coming here, to this island, to the monastery, was a rite of expurgation. He did not want to live in a world where one's virtues are negotiable, yet he desired a permanence divided from God. Shipwrecked, lost, he had about him the nobility of a man on his deathbed when he arrived."

The afternoon light sharpened the colors of the day, polished the white of the flagstones on which we stood. The monk came closer to me.

"Often we would stand like this," he said, "Nikola and I, overlooking the island. I would tell him to look at the live vitality of all that is below us and let that be a reflection of all that is above. What need is there for words? Even on earth our vision is greater than our speech. Let the beauty of the natural world fill your soul with wonder and faith, and let it cancel your doubt. You are not an exile in this world, I said. This beauty is the reality to which my faith is anchored. Let this be your anchor too, I told him. God is reality, and reality is God. God is below us and above us, and God is all around us, obvious and profound, like the beat of your heart."

"What did he say?"

"What he said changed with his mood. Sometimes I feel he believed me, saw what I saw. Other times he was bitter and said that a man who awakes without a doubt in what he believes is living an illusion. If amused, he would tell me how his father, a doctor and a believer in God, told him that, like a man of science, a man of religion should never offer guarantees. But once Nikola said that to apprehend reality one must be in perfect harmony with the world, which for an exile like him was impossible. He said this not long before he left, as a sort of last word on the subject, a final admission of defeat. It was as though every thought of Nikola's was an exercise of doubt, as though thought and doubt were for him one and the same."

"My father too was a doctor," I said.

"I'm sure you and Nikola have much in common. Otherwise why would you have come? Here, let me show you the room in which he stayed, Muhamed. It is bare now but there is perhaps still present within those four walls some ineffable trace of him."

The room to which the monk showed me is the room I'm writing from now. I will stay here for a while. There are four of us in this monastery, three monks and I, and now I do the work Nikola had done. Above the door, written in black paint, it says, simply, "I am the door." Something about this phrase stirs me. There is a deep peace and silence, and a deep emptiness, on this island and in this monastery. Not the silence of nothingness, but the silence of being in peaceful contemplation of the possibility of nothingness.

I have not written to Stefan. What is there to write? After I finish this, the story of my exile, I will write no more. My travels, like those of Nikola, were not a quest for redemption but a series of reactions, something much more human, and much less noble. This is the true story of exile, as old as the tale of Odysseus, who was but a pawn of the gods as surely as Nikola and I are the pawns of history and fate.

I wonder if Nikola, as he traveled from land to land, ever doubted the continuity of the self through time and space. Did he become a stranger, an exile, even to himself? If doubt blurs the borders that certainty erects, as the monk told me, then it blurs too the borders of one's being.

I imagine Nikola waiting at the pier for the ship that took him from this island and back toward the world. If I did see him then, I must have confused him for a miner. He too, if he had seen me, must have confused me for someone else.

Acknowledgements

Some of the stories have appeared or will appear in the following publications: "A Brief History of the Southern Slavs" in *Denver Quarterly*; "Deathwinked" in *American Fiction: The Best Unpublished Stories by Emerging Writers* and *Electric Literature's Recommended Reading*; "Documentary" in *Mississippi Review*; "Witness to a Prayer" in *The Collagist*; "The Poet from Mostar" in *CutBank*; "Translated from the Bosnian" in *Blackbird*; "Admir and Benjamin" in *North American Review*; "Hand in Glove" in *The Massachusetts Review*; "Like Coming Home" in *Witness*; and "The Exile of Muhamed Mehmedbašić" in *The Gettysburg Review*.

Vedran Husić was born in Bosnia and Herzegovina and raised in Germany and the United States. He has work published in *The Gettysburg Review, The Massachusetts Review, Mississippi Review, Witness, Ecotone, Electric Literature's Recommended Reading,* and elsewhere. He is the recipient of fellowships from the Fine Arts Work Center in Provincetown and the National Endowment for the Arts.

Printed in the USA
CPSIA information can be obtained
at www.ICGtesting.com
LVHW052153061123
763231LV00004B/405